TAO
The Little Samurai

#3

Clowns and Dragons!

Laurent Richard
illustrated by Nicolas Ryser
Translation: Edward Gauvin

Graphic Universe™ • Minneapolis

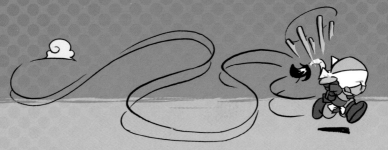

STORY BY LAURENT RICHARD
ILLUSTRATIONS BY NICOLAS RYSER
TRANSLATION BY EDWARD GAUVIN

FIRST AMERICAN EDITION PUBLISHED IN 2014 BY GRAPHIC UNIVERSE™.

PITRES ET DRAGONS! BY LAURENT RICHARD AND NICOLAS RYSER © BAYARD ÉDITIONS, 2011
COPYRIGHT © 2014 BY LERNER PUBLISHING GROUP, INC., FOR THE US EDITION

GRAPHIC UNIVERSE™ IS A TRADEMARK OF LERNER PUBLISHING GROUP, INC.

GRAPHIC UNIVERSE™
A DIVISION OF LERNER PUBLISHING GROUP, INC.
241 FIRST AVENUE NORTH
MINNEAPOLIS, MN 55401 USA

FOR READING LEVELS AND MORE INFORMATION,
LOOK UP THIS TITLE AT WWW.LERNERBOOKS.COM.

MAIN BODY TEXT SET IN CCWILDWORDS 8.5/10.5.
TYPEFACE PROVIDED BY FONTOGRAPHER.

LIBRARY OF CONGRESS CATALOGING-IN-PUBLICATION DATA

RICHARD, LAURENT, 1968-
    [PITRES ET DRAGONS! ENGLISH.]
    CLOWNS AND DRAGONS! / LAURENT RICHARD ; ILLUSTRATED BY NICOLAS RYSER ; TRANSLATION,
EDWARD GAUVIN. – FIRST AMERICAN EDITION.
        P.   CM. – (TAO, THE LITTLE SAMURAI ; #3)
    SUMMARY: TAO IS A FEARLESS SAMURAI APPRENTICE STUDYING TO BECOME A VIRTUOSO MARTIAL
ARTIST. BUT WHEN YOU'RE NATURALLY GOOD AT PRANKS, PRACTICAL JOKES, AND OTHER SILLY
ANTICS (INCLUDING TRYING TO TEACH KUNG FU MOVES TO THE BIG, LAZY CAT, BRUCE LEE), IT'S
HARD TO CONCENTRATE ON LEARNING HOW TO SLAY DRAGONS.
    ISBN 978-1-4677-2096-0 (LIB. BDG. : ALK. PAPER)
    ISBN 978-1-4677-2555-2 (EBOOK)
    1. GRAPHIC NOVELS. [1. GRAPHIC NOVELS. 2. MARTIAL ARTS-FICTION. 3. SAMURAI-FICTION.
4. SCHOOLS-FICTION. 5. BEHAVIOR-FICTION.] I. RYSER, NICOLAS, ILLUSTRATOR. II. GAUVIN,
EDWARD, TRANSLATOR. III. TITLE.
PZ7.7.R5CL 2014
741.5'944–DC23   2013027734

MANUFACTURED IN THE UNITED STATES OF AMERICA
1 – VI – 12/31/13

Fortune Favors the Archer

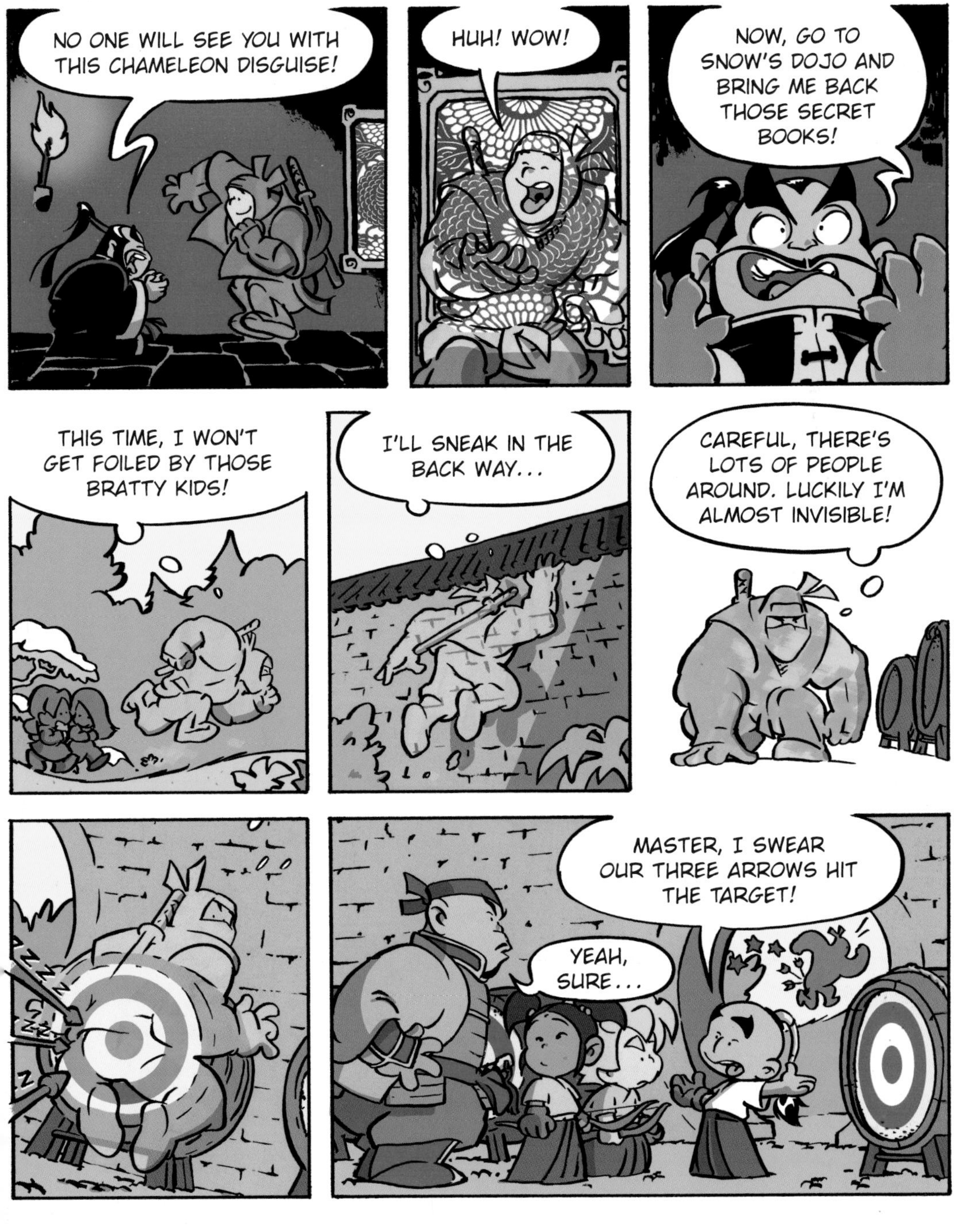
NO ONE WILL SEE YOU WITH THIS CHAMELEON DISGUISE!
HUH! WOW!
NOW, GO TO SNOW'S DOJO AND BRING ME BACK THOSE SECRET BOOKS!
THIS TIME, I WON'T GET FOILED BY THOSE BRATTY KIDS!
I'LL SNEAK IN THE BACK WAY...
CAREFUL, THERE'S LOTS OF PEOPLE AROUND. LUCKILY I'M ALMOST INVISIBLE!
MASTER, I SWEAR OUR THREE ARROWS HIT THE TARGET!
YEAH, SURE...

Never Be an Absent-Minded Cheater

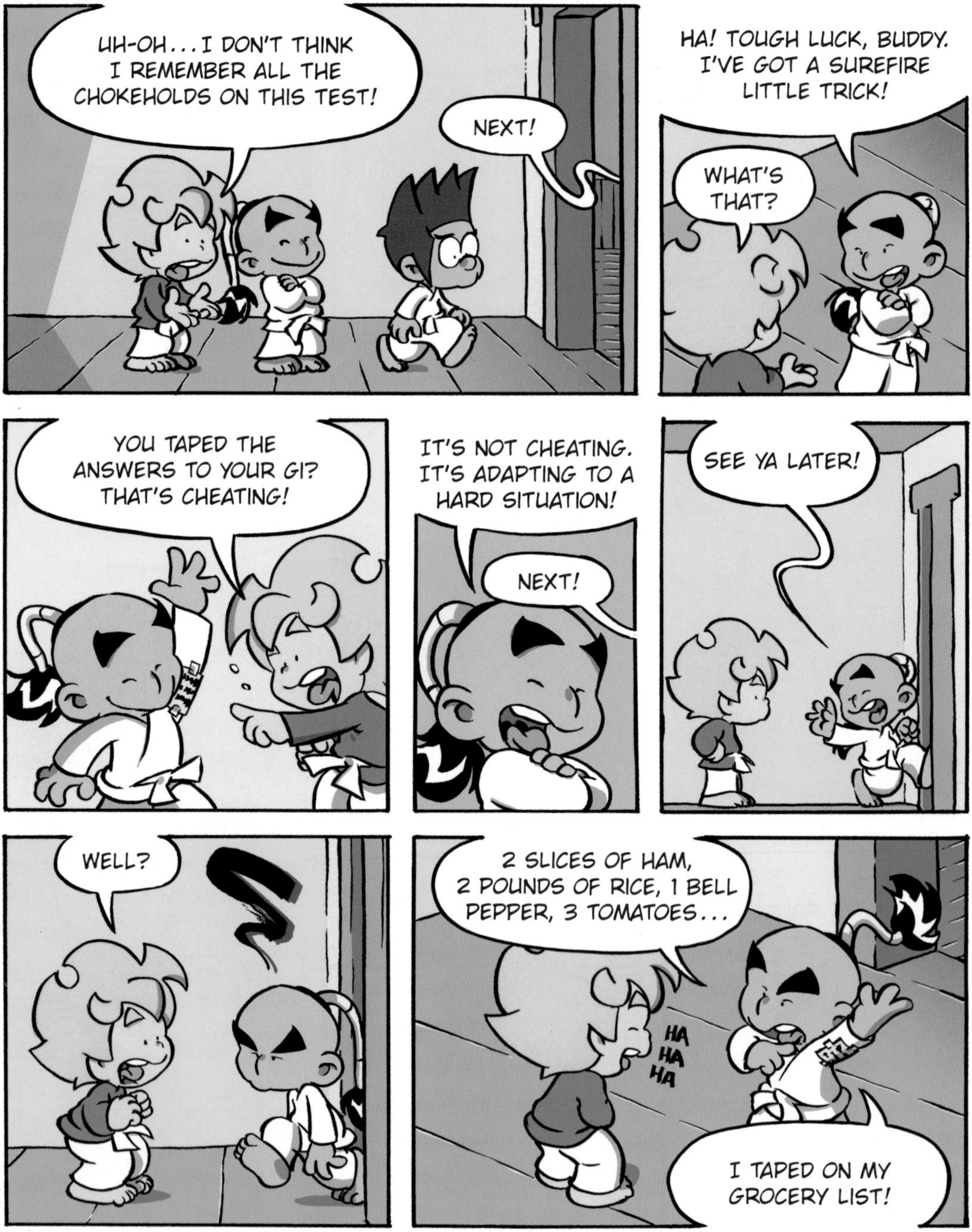

UH-OH . . . I DON'T THINK I REMEMBER ALL THE CHOKEHOLDS ON THIS TEST!
NEXT!
HA! TOUGH LUCK, BUDDY. I'VE GOT A SUREFIRE LITTLE TRICK!
WHAT'S THAT?
YOU TAPED THE ANSWERS TO YOUR GI? THAT'S CHEATING!
IT'S NOT CHEATING. IT'S ADAPTING TO A HARD SITUATION!
NEXT!
SEE YA LATER!
WELL?
2 SLICES OF HAM, 2 POUNDS OF RICE, 1 BELL PEPPER, 3 TOMATOES . . .
HA HA HA
I TAPED ON MY GROCERY LIST!

Look Before You Leap

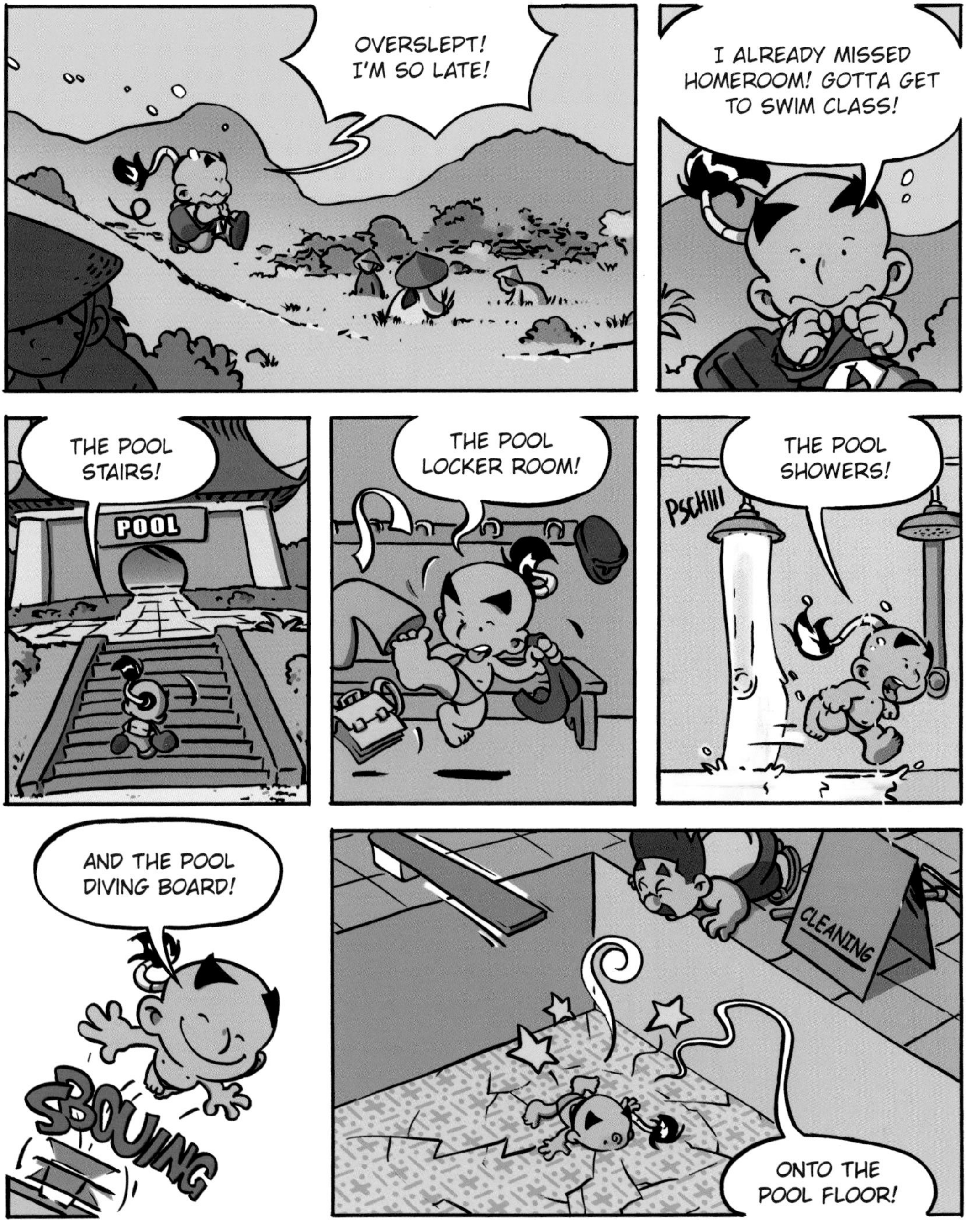
OVERSLEPT! I'M SO LATE!
I ALREADY MISSED HOMEROOM! GOTTA GET TO SWIM CLASS!
THE POOL STAIRS!
POOL
THE POOL LOCKER ROOM!
THE POOL SHOWERS!
PSCHIII
AND THE POOL DIVING BOARD!
SBOUING
CLEANING
ONTO THE POOL FLOOR!

Sweet Revenge Brings Tears to Your Eyes

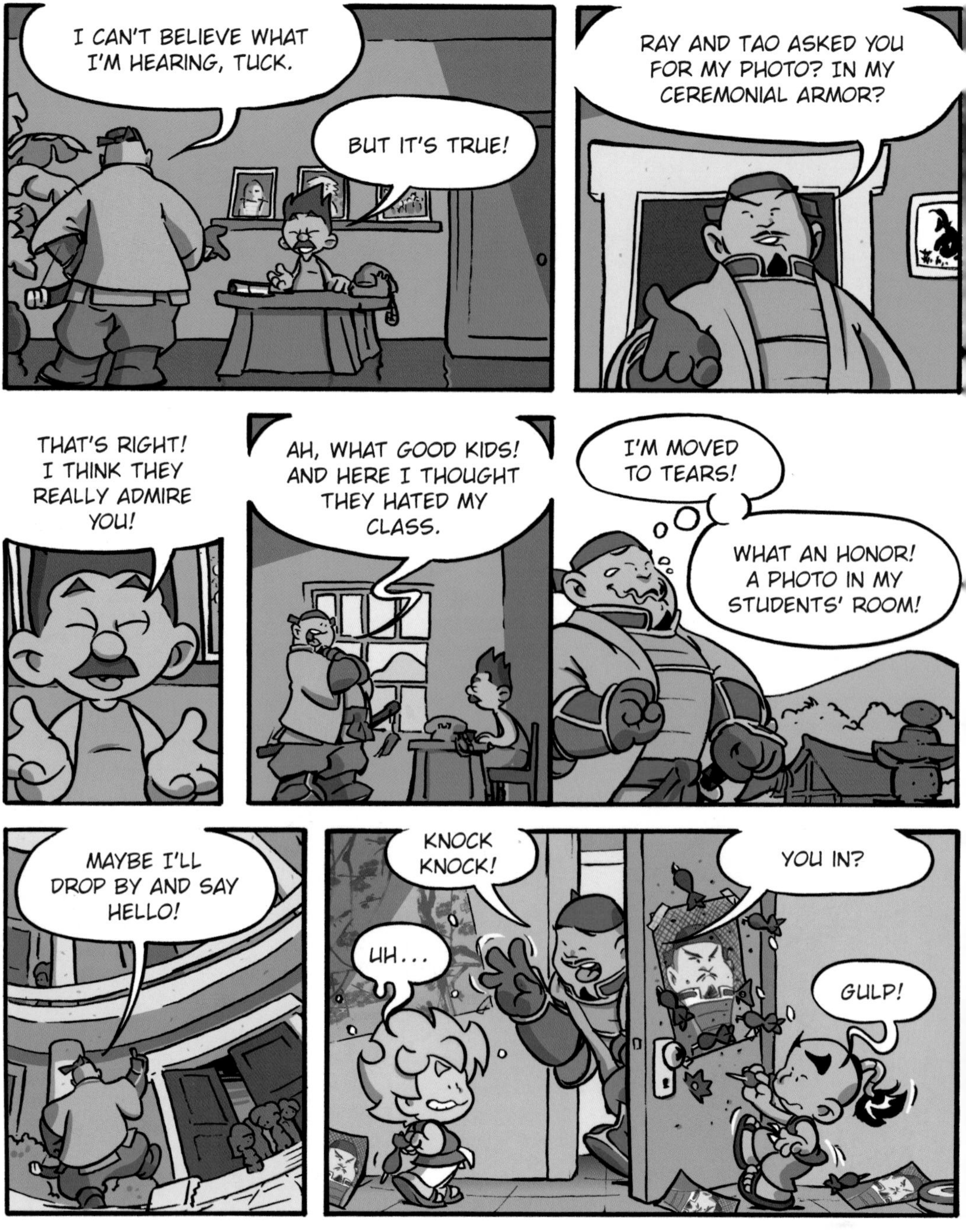
I CAN'T BELIEVE WHAT I'M HEARING, TUCK.
BUT IT'S TRUE!
RAY AND TAO ASKED YOU FOR MY PHOTO? IN MY CEREMONIAL ARMOR?
THAT'S RIGHT! I THINK THEY REALLY ADMIRE YOU!
AH, WHAT GOOD KIDS! AND HERE I THOUGHT THEY HATED MY CLASS.
I'M MOVED TO TEARS!
WHAT AN HONOR! A PHOTO IN MY STUDENTS' ROOM!
MAYBE I'LL DROP BY AND SAY HELLO!
KNOCK KNOCK!
YOU IN?
UH...
GULP!

A Samurai in Love

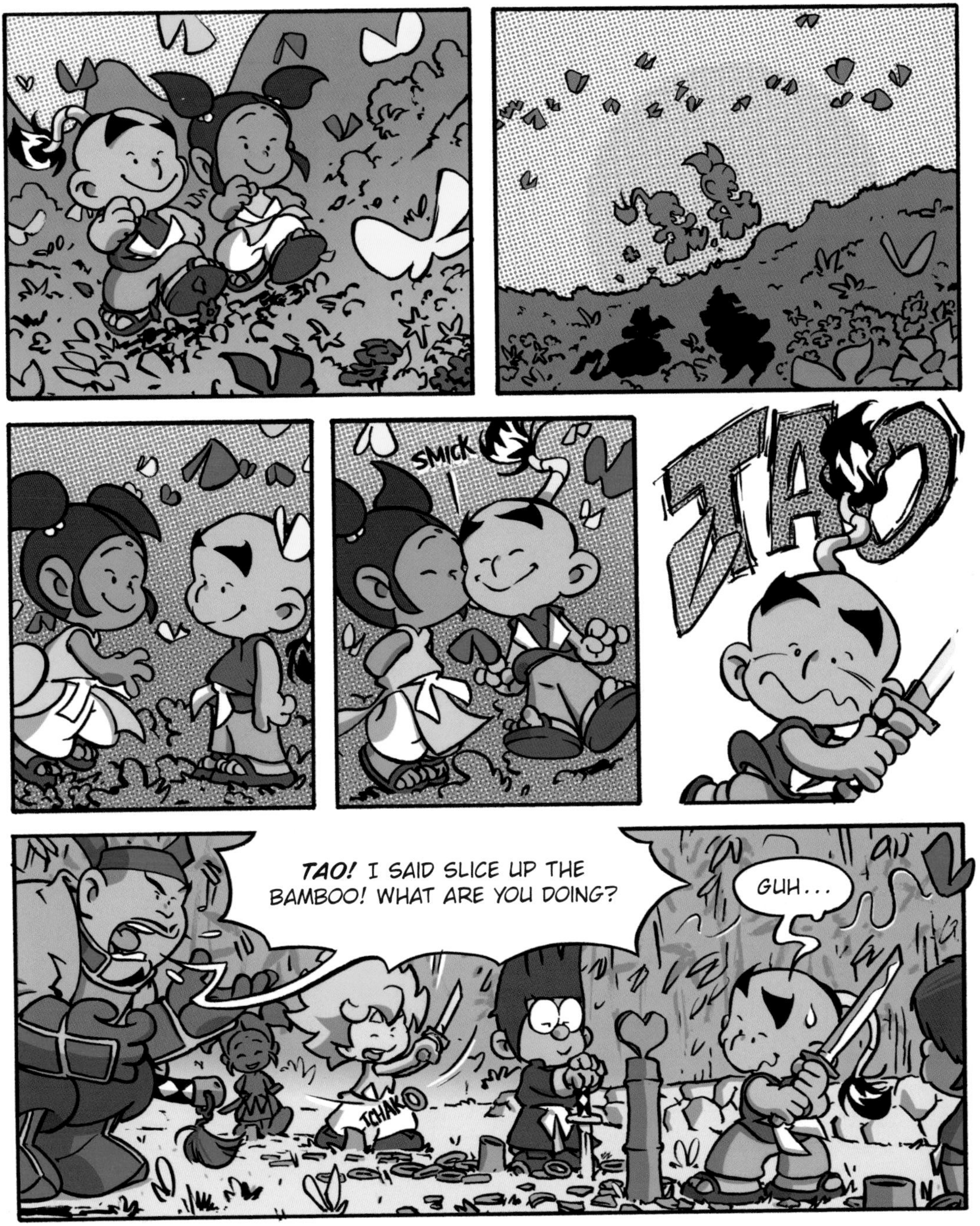
SMICK
TAO
TAO! I SAID SLICE UP THE BAMBOO! WHAT ARE YOU DOING?
ICHAKO
GUH...

Practice Makes Train Wreck

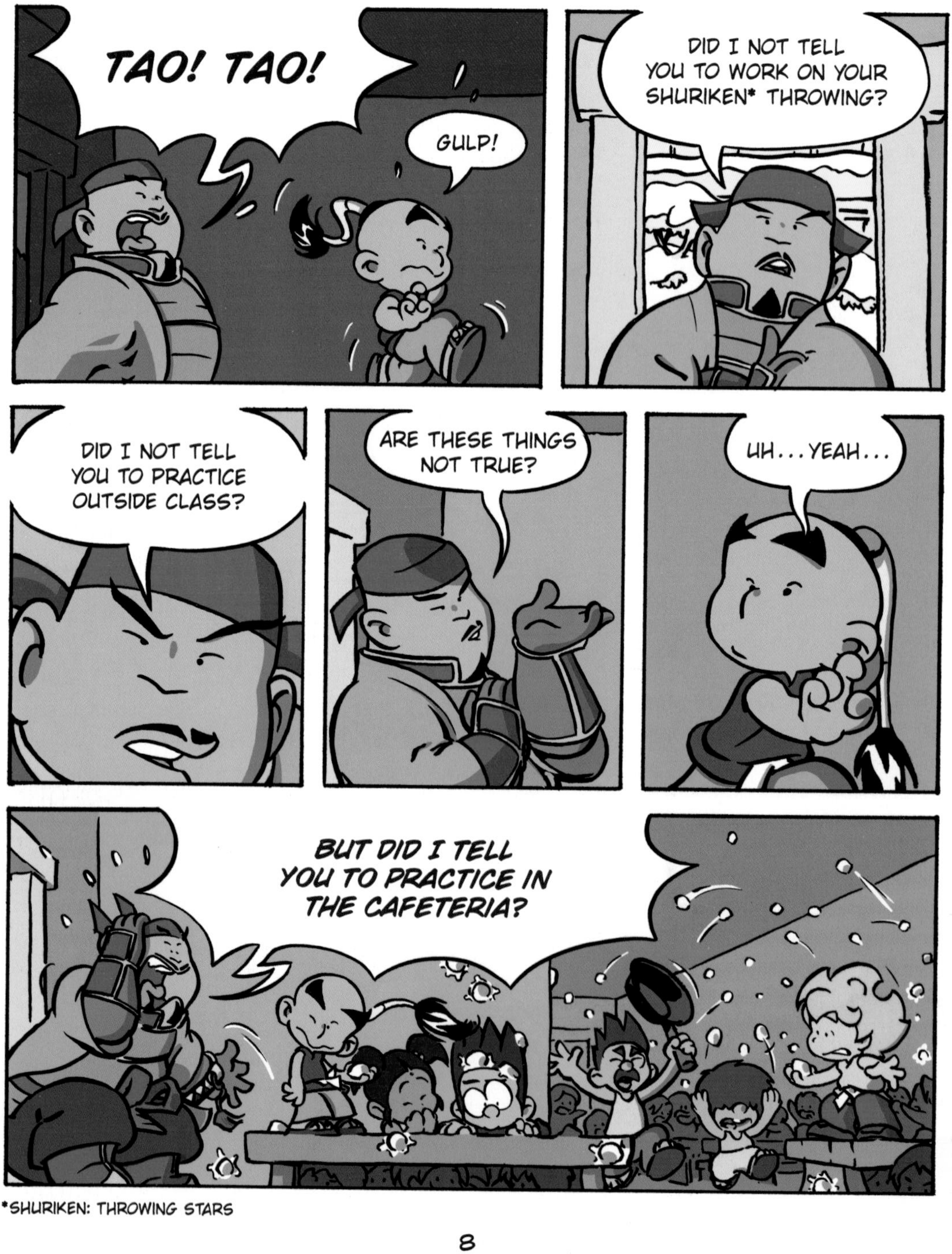
TAO! TAO!
GULP!
DID I NOT TELL YOU TO WORK ON YOUR SHURIKEN* THROWING?
DID I NOT TELL YOU TO PRACTICE OUTSIDE CLASS?
ARE THESE THINGS NOT TRUE?
UH... YEAH...
BUT DID I TELL YOU TO PRACTICE IN THE CAFETERIA?

*SHURIKEN: THROWING STARS

The Little Samurai Is Like a Bamboo Shoot

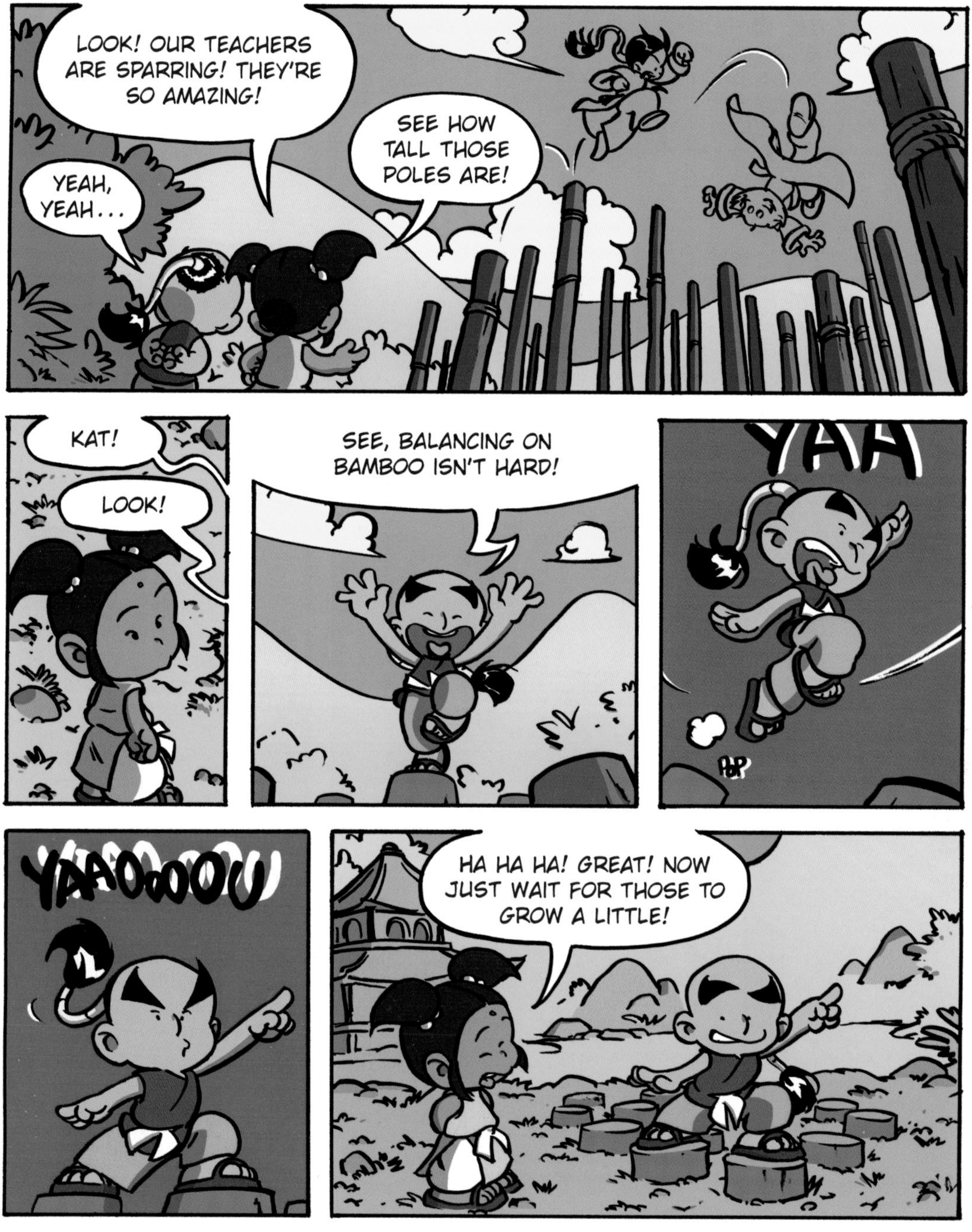
LOOK! OUR TEACHERS ARE SPARRING! THEY'RE SO AMAZING!
YEAH, YEAH...
SEE HOW TALL THOSE POLES ARE!
KAT!
LOOK!
SEE, BALANCING ON BAMBOO ISN'T HARD!
YAA
HOP
YAAOOOOU
HA HA HA! GREAT! NOW JUST WAIT FOR THOSE TO GROW A LITTLE!

A Walk in the Woods

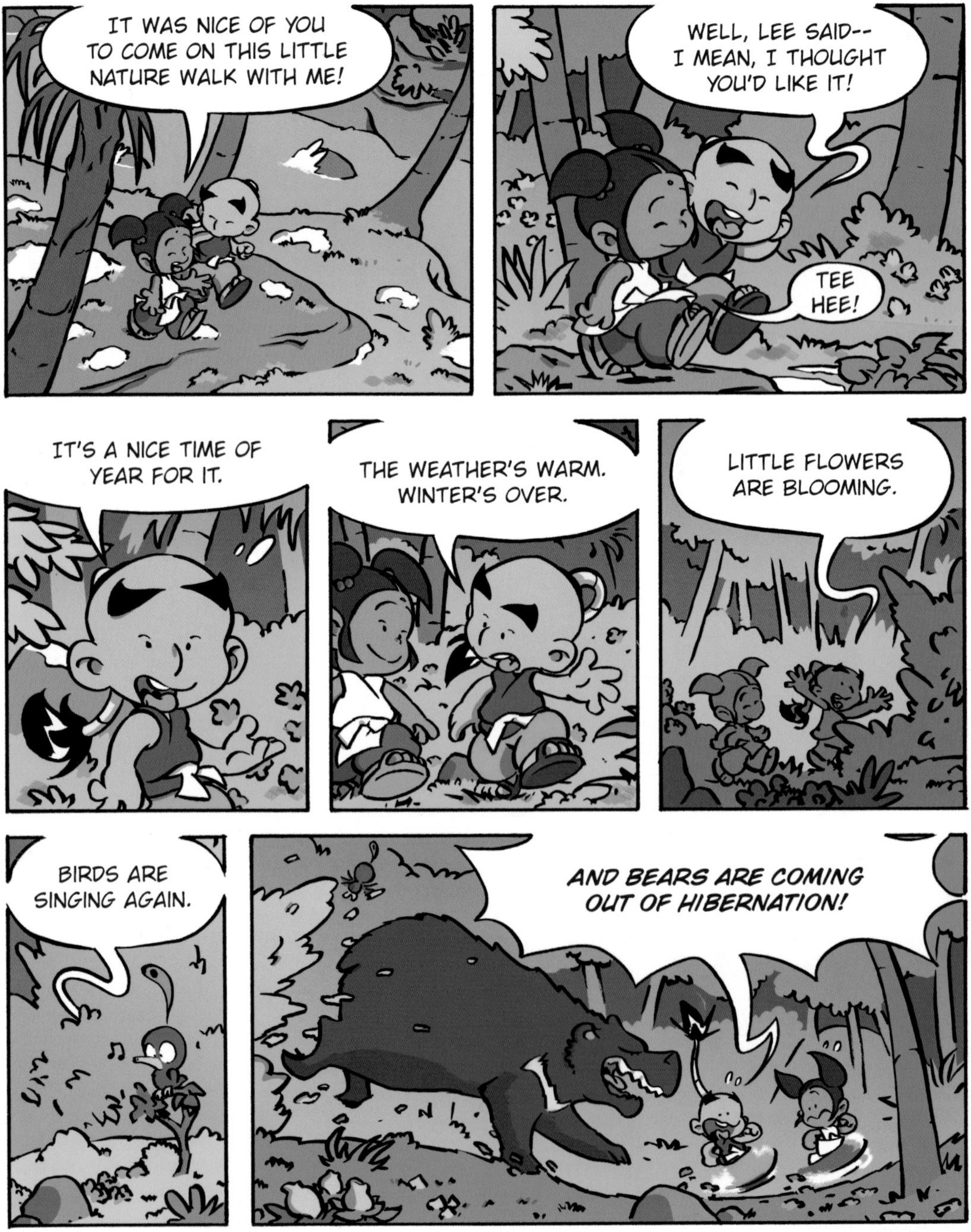
IT WAS NICE OF YOU TO COME ON THIS LITTLE NATURE WALK WITH ME!
WELL, LEE SAID-- I MEAN, I THOUGHT YOU'D LIKE IT!
TEE HEE!
IT'S A NICE TIME OF YEAR FOR IT.
THE WEATHER'S WARM. WINTER'S OVER.
LITTLE FLOWERS ARE BLOOMING.
BIRDS ARE SINGING AGAIN.
AND BEARS ARE COMING OUT OF HIBERNATION!

A Grasshopper's Eyes Are Bigger Than His Stomach

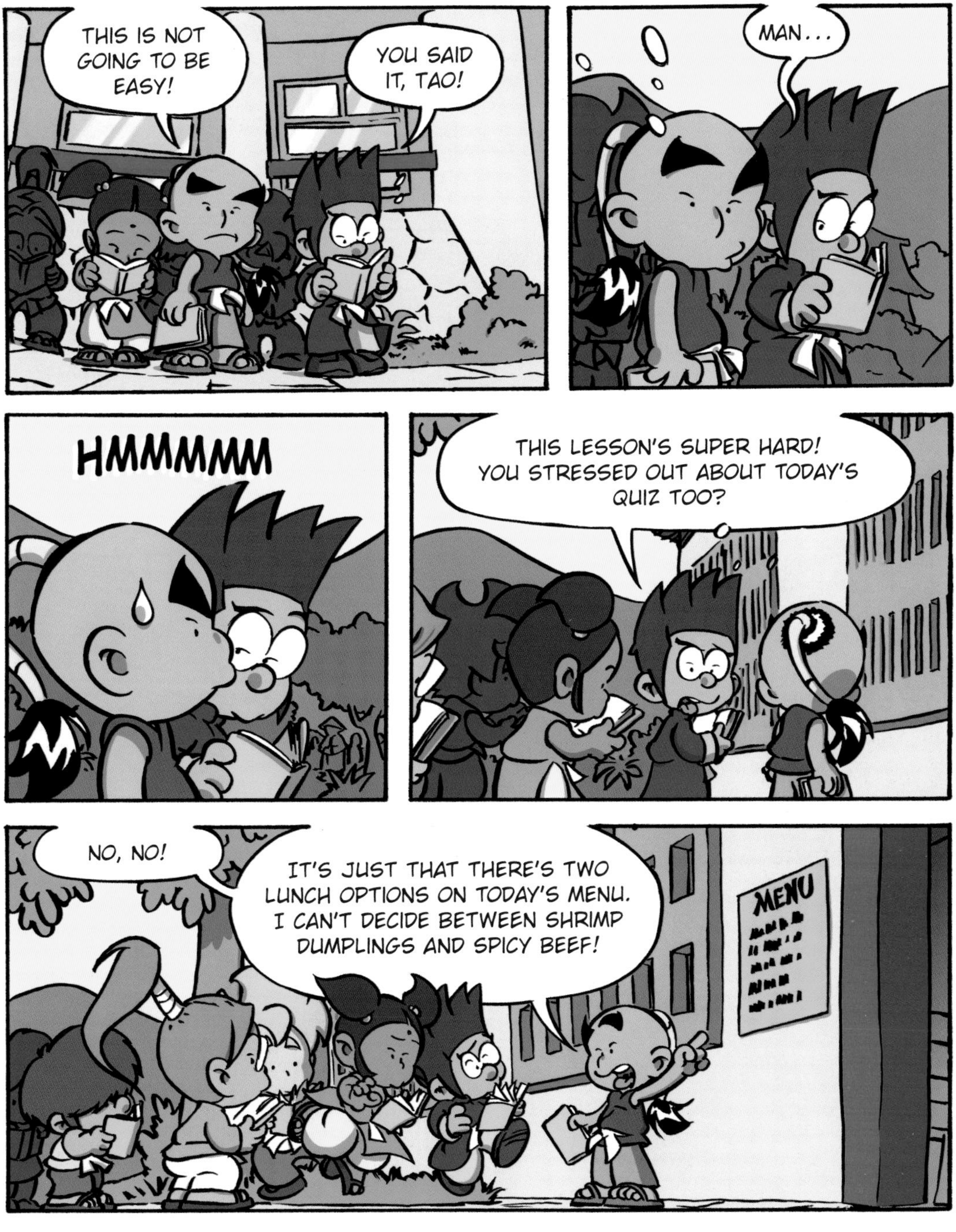
THIS IS NOT GOING TO BE EASY!
YOU SAID IT, TAO!
MAN...
HMMMMM
THIS LESSON'S SUPER HARD! YOU STRESSED OUT ABOUT TODAY'S QUIZ TOO?
NO, NO!
IT'S JUST THAT THERE'S TWO LUNCH OPTIONS ON TODAY'S MENU. I CAN'T DECIDE BETWEEN SHRIMP DUMPLINGS AND SPICY BEEF!
MENU

Sugar Rush

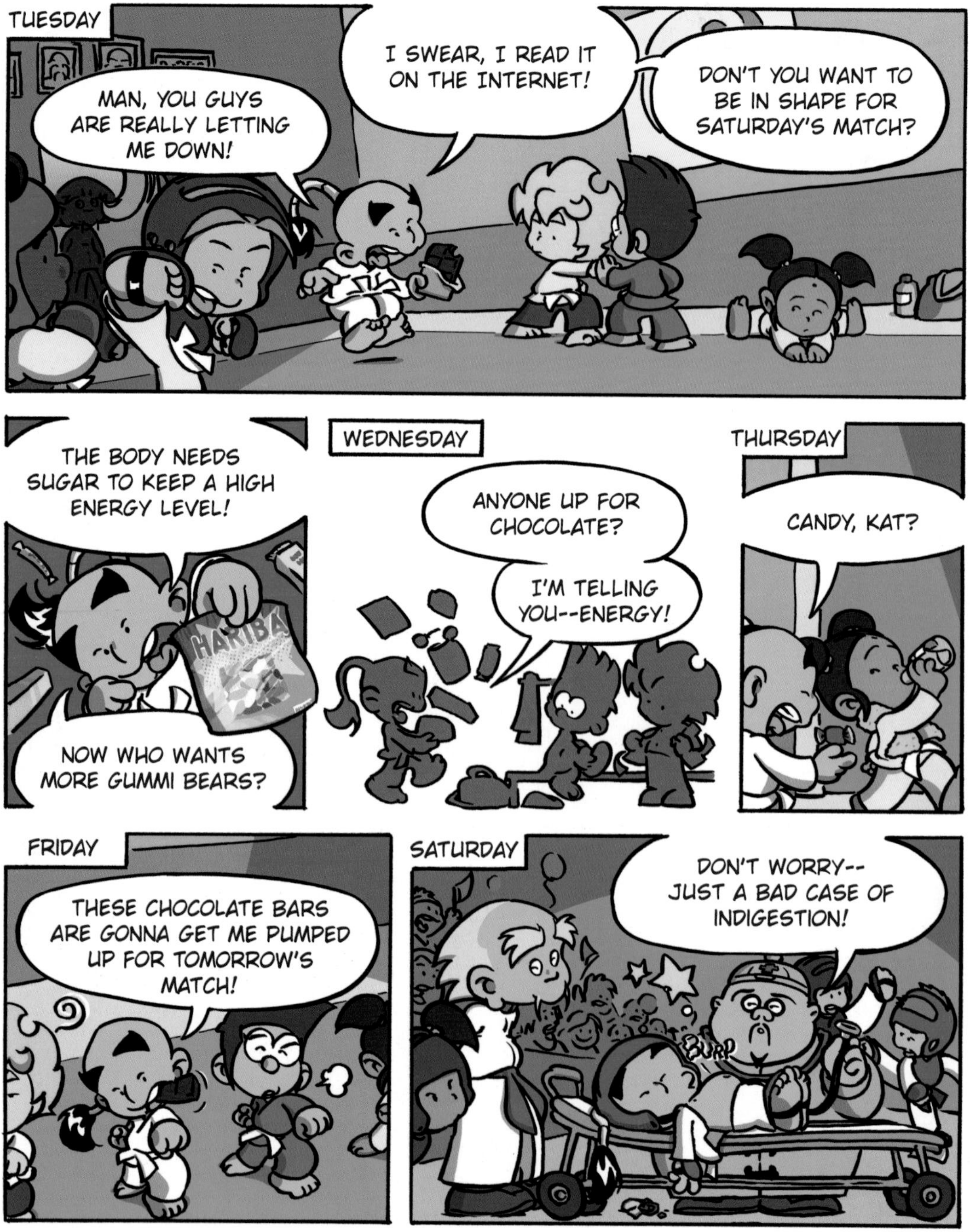
TUESDAY
MAN, YOU GUYS ARE REALLY LETTING ME DOWN!
I SWEAR, I READ IT ON THE INTERNET!
DON'T YOU WANT TO BE IN SHAPE FOR SATURDAY'S MATCH?
THE BODY NEEDS SUGAR TO KEEP A HIGH ENERGY LEVEL!
NOW WHO WANTS MORE GUMMI BEARS?
WEDNESDAY
ANYONE UP FOR CHOCOLATE?
I'M TELLING YOU--ENERGY!
THURSDAY
CANDY, KAT?
FRIDAY
THESE CHOCOLATE BARS ARE GONNA GET ME PUMPED UP FOR TOMORROW'S MATCH!
SATURDAY
DON'T WORRY-- JUST A BAD CASE OF INDIGESTION!
BURP

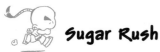

A Grasshopper Needs Good Study Habits

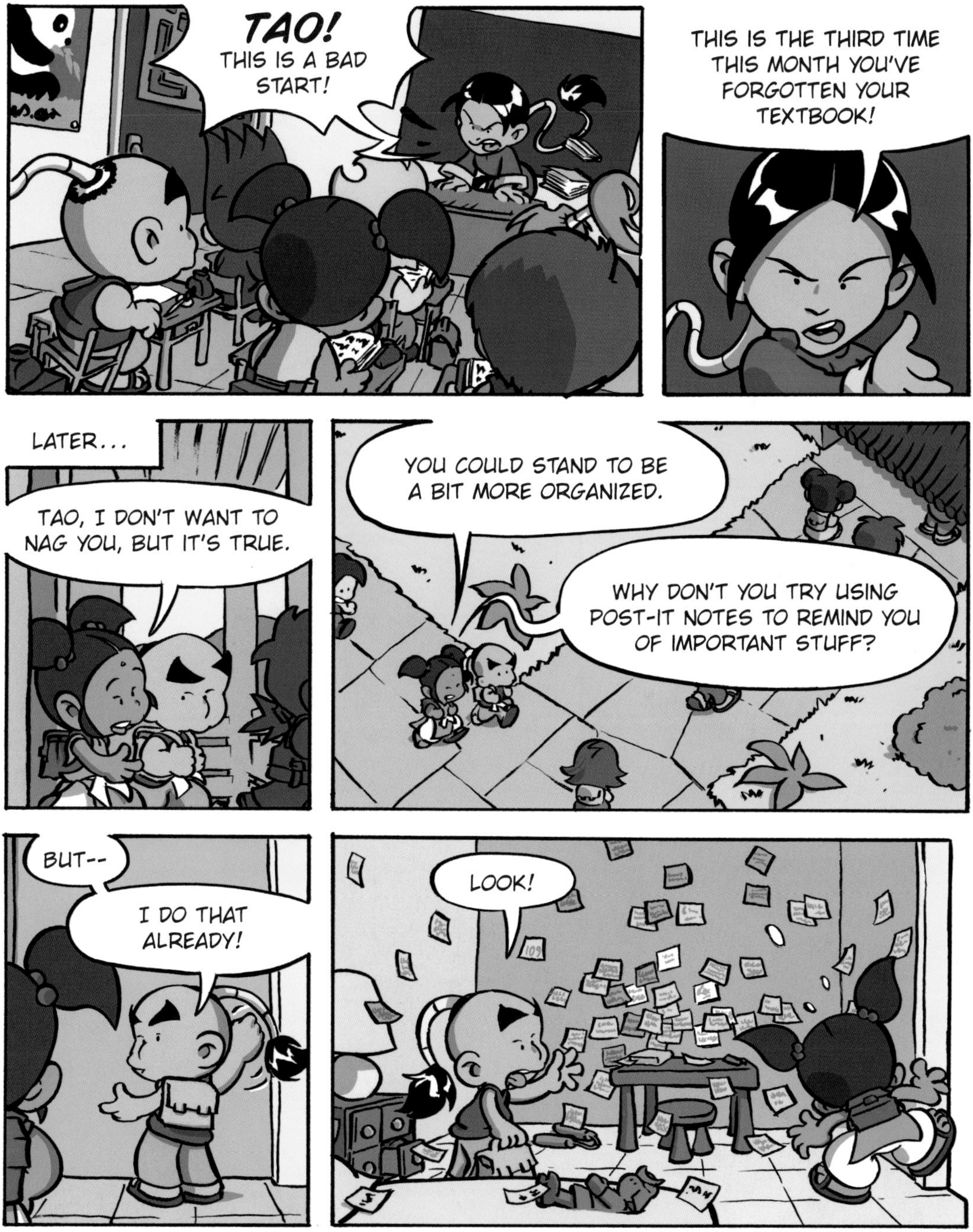

TAO! THIS IS A BAD START!
THIS IS THE THIRD TIME THIS MONTH YOU'VE FORGOTTEN YOUR TEXTBOOK!
LATER...
TAO, I DON'T WANT TO NAG YOU, BUT IT'S TRUE.
YOU COULD STAND TO BE A BIT MORE ORGANIZED.
WHY DON'T YOU TRY USING POST-IT NOTES TO REMIND YOU OF IMPORTANT STUFF?
BUT--
I DO THAT ALREADY!
LOOK!

Sculpture Comes Easy to a Samurai Master

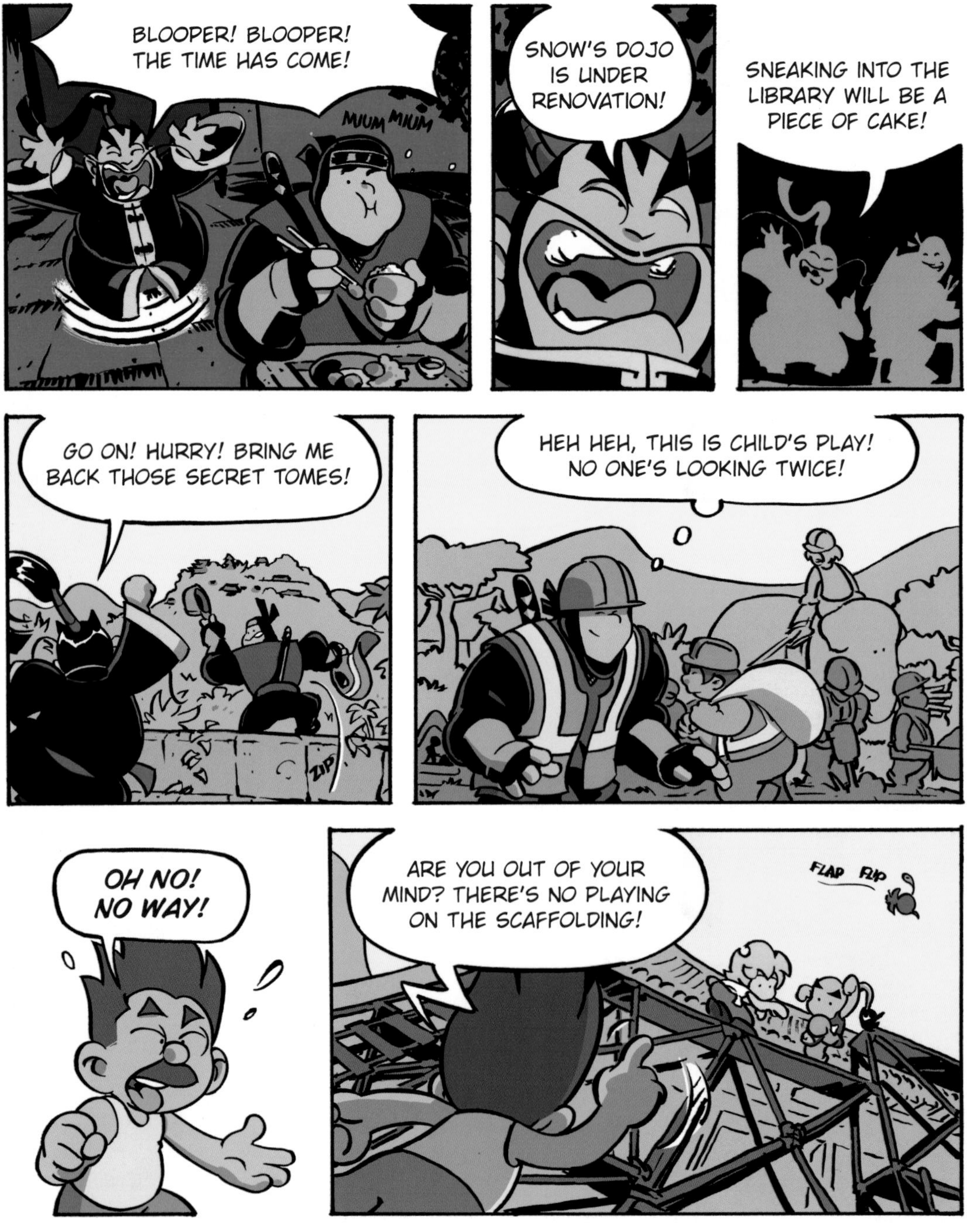
BLOOPER! BLOOPER! THE TIME HAS COME!
MIUM MIUM
SNOW'S DOJO IS UNDER RENOVATION!
SNEAKING INTO THE LIBRARY WILL BE A PIECE OF CAKE!
GO ON! HURRY! BRING ME BACK THOSE SECRET TOMES!
ZIP!
HEH HEH, THIS IS CHILD'S PLAY! NO ONE'S LOOKING TWICE!
OH NO! NO WAY!
ARE YOU OUT OF YOUR MIND? THERE'S NO PLAYING ON THE SCAFFOLDING!
FLAP FLIP

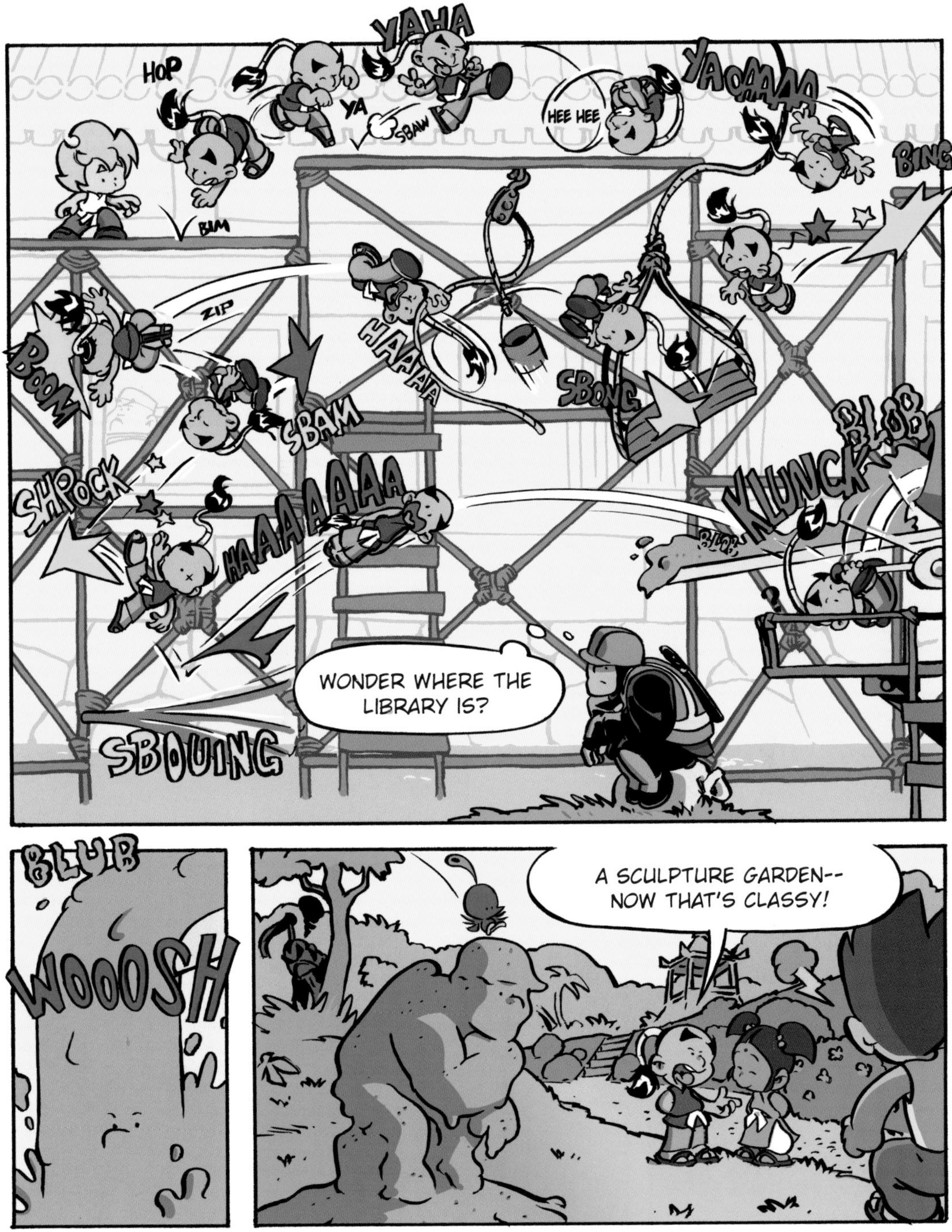
HOP
YAHA
YA
SBAM
HEE HEE
YAOAAAA
BING
BIM
ZIP
BOOM
HAAAAA
SBAM
SBONG
BLOB
SHPOCK
HAAAAAAAA
KLUNCK
WONDER WHERE THE LIBRARY IS?
SBOUING
BLUB
WOOOSH
A SCULPTURE GARDEN-- NOW THAT'S CLASSY!

The Smallest Fly Can Break a Silence

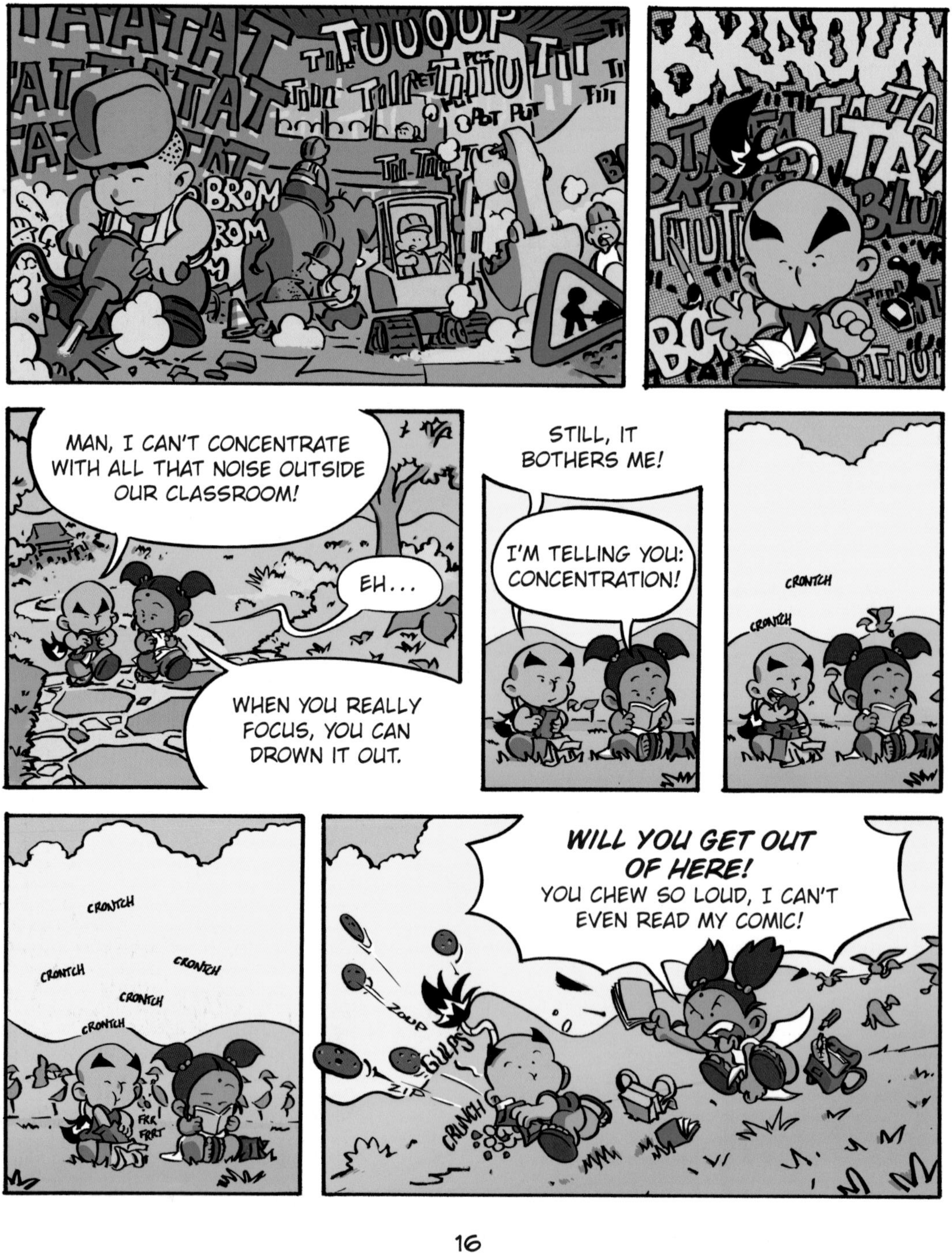
TATATAT
TUUUUP
TIII
TIIIIU
POT PUT
BROM
ROM
TATA
TAT
MAN, I CAN'T CONCENTRATE WITH ALL THAT NOISE OUTSIDE OUR CLASSROOM!
EH...
WHEN YOU REALLY FOCUS, YOU CAN DROWN IT OUT.
STILL, IT BOTHERS ME!
I'M TELLING YOU: CONCENTRATION!
CRONTCH
CRONTCH
CRONTCH
CRONTCH
CRONTCH
CRONTCH
CRONTCH
FRR FRRT
WILL YOU GET OUT OF HERE!
YOU CHEW SO LOUD, I CAN'T EVEN READ MY COMIC!
ZOUP
GULPS
ZIP
CRUNCH

Cannonball!

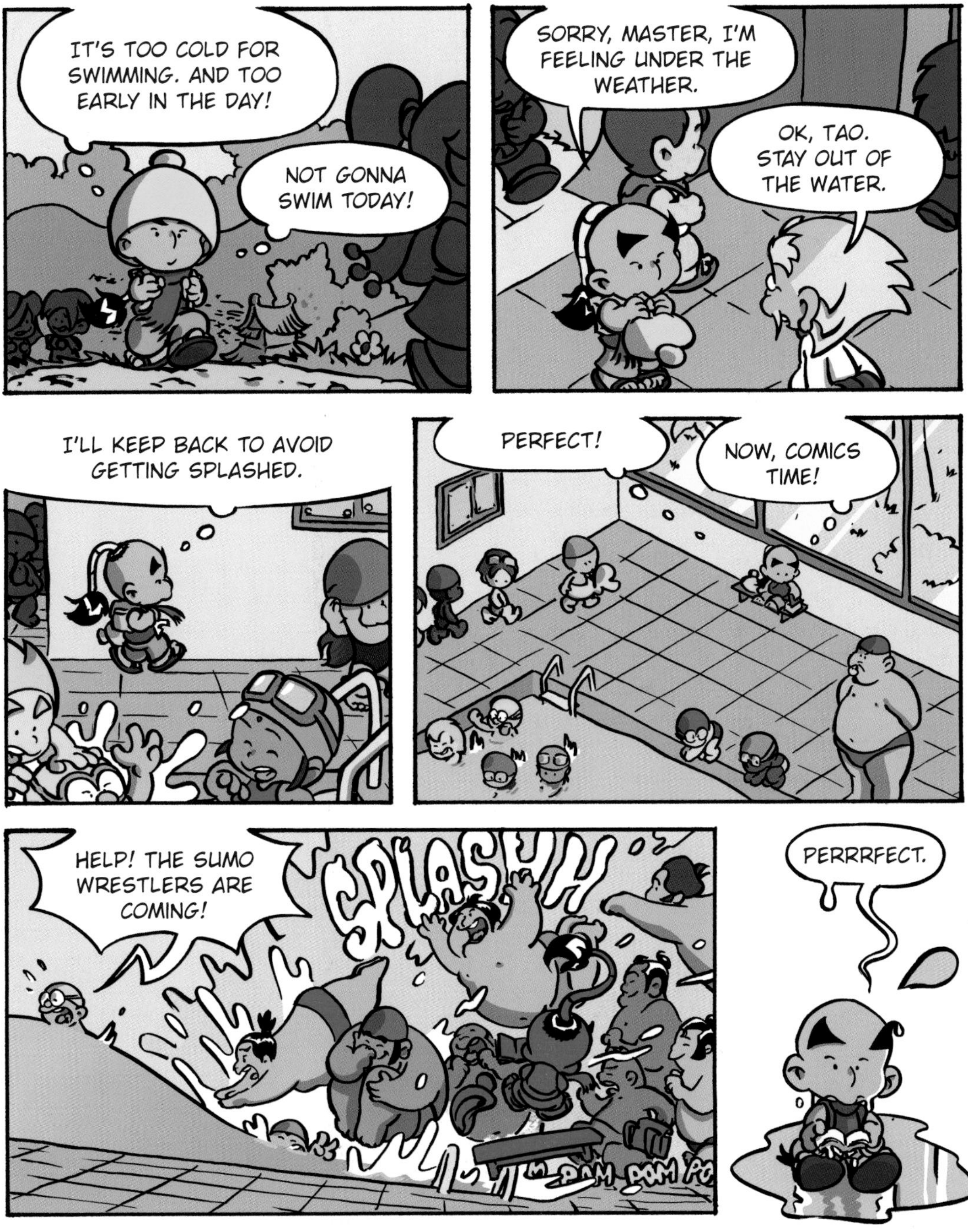
IT'S TOO COLD FOR SWIMMING. AND TOO EARLY IN THE DAY!
NOT GONNA SWIM TODAY!
SORRY, MASTER, I'M FEELING UNDER THE WEATHER.
OK, TAO. STAY OUT OF THE WATER.
I'LL KEEP BACK TO AVOID GETTING SPLASHED.
PERFECT!
NOW, COMICS TIME!
HELP! THE SUMO WRESTLERS ARE COMING!
POM POM PO
PERRRFECT.

A Web-Footed Warrior

HA HA! LEFT THOSE FISHIES IN THE DUST!

 WHO'S THE FLIPPER KING?

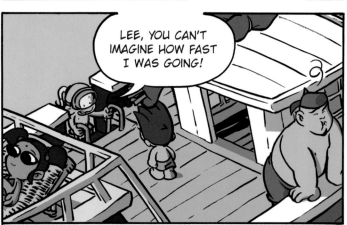

LEE, YOU CAN'T IMAGINE HOW FAST I WAS GOING!

MAN, I'M HUNGRY! COME DOWN FOR A SNACK WITH ME. I'LL TELL YOU ALL ABOUT IT!

SURE, BUT UH--

YOU SHOULD TAKE YOUR FLIPPERS OFF!

A Samurai Knows What He Wants

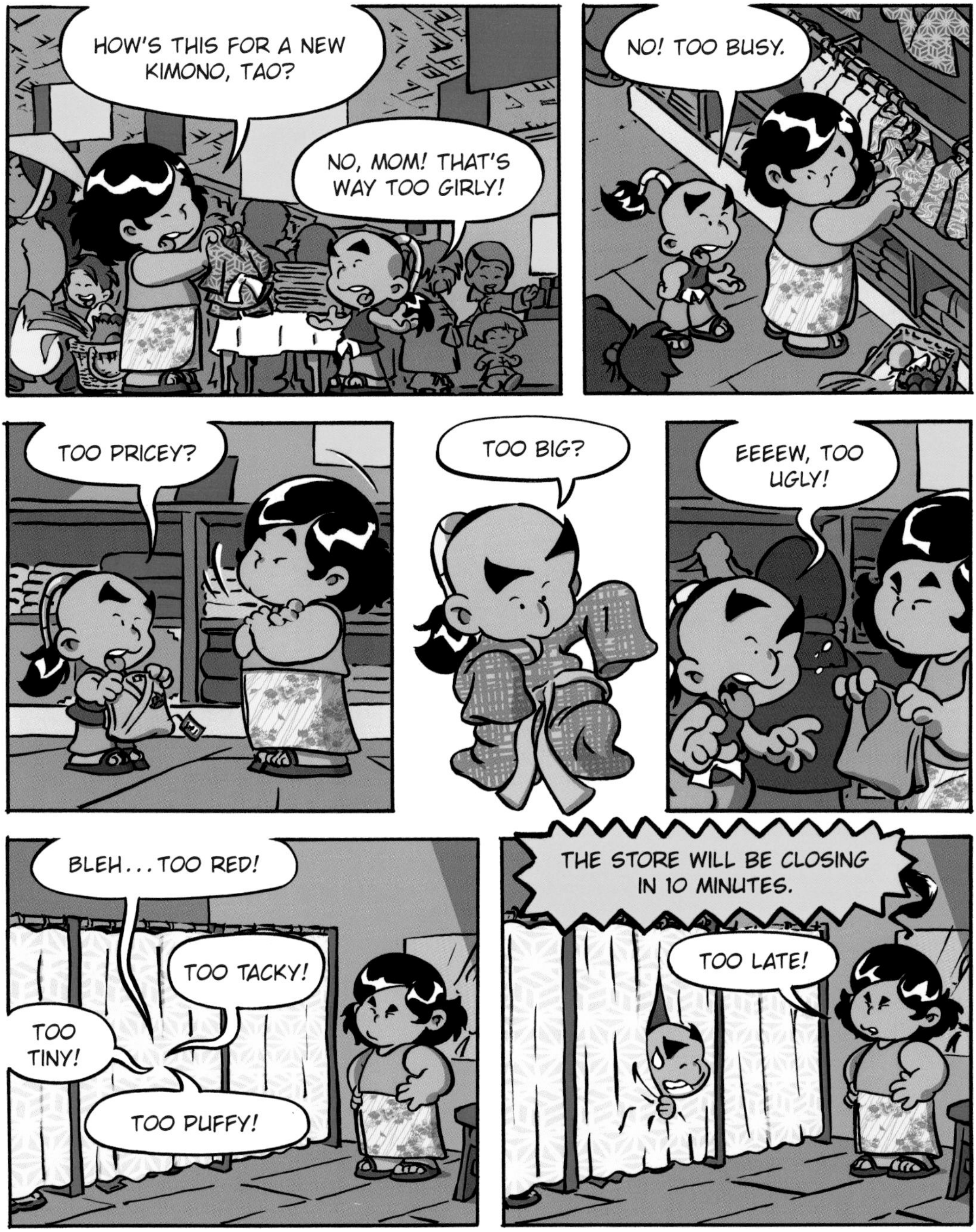
HOW'S THIS FOR A NEW KIMONO, TAO?
NO, MOM! THAT'S WAY TOO GIRLY!
NO! TOO BUSY.
TOO PRICEY?
TOO BIG?
EEEEW, TOO UGLY!
BLEH... TOO RED!
TOO TACKY!
TOO TINY!
TOO PUFFY!
THE STORE WILL BE CLOSING IN 10 MINUTES.
TOO LATE!

The Grasshopper Learns to Leave on Time

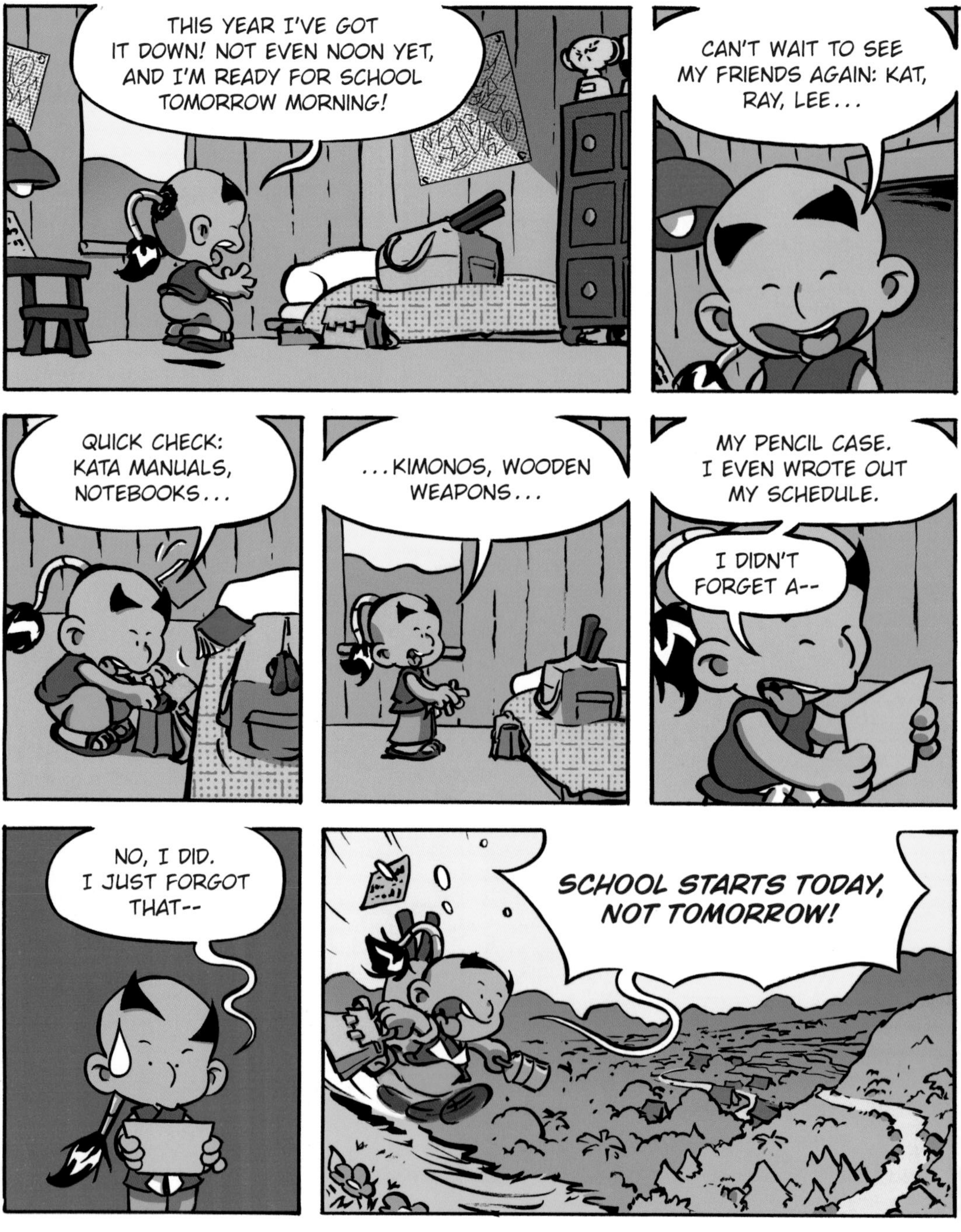
THIS YEAR I'VE GOT IT DOWN! NOT EVEN NOON YET, AND I'M READY FOR SCHOOL TOMORROW MORNING!
CAN'T WAIT TO SEE MY FRIENDS AGAIN: KAT, RAY, LEE...
QUICK CHECK: KATA MANUALS, NOTEBOOKS...
...KIMONOS, WOODEN WEAPONS...
MY PENCIL CASE. I EVEN WROTE OUT MY SCHEDULE.
I DIDN'T FORGET A--
NO, I DID. I JUST FORGOT THAT--
SCHOOL STARTS TODAY, NOT TOMORROW!

The Ninja Envies the Chameleon

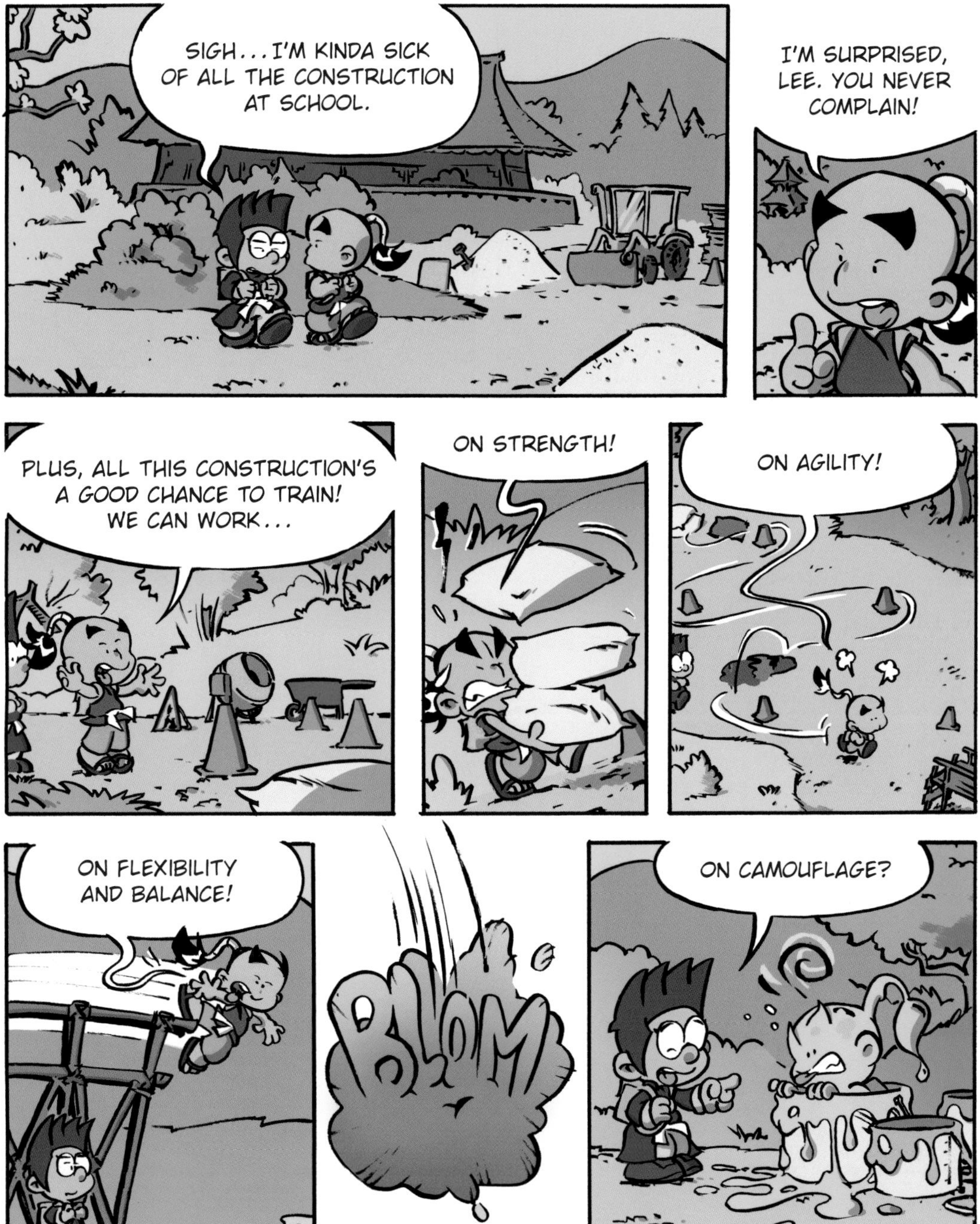
SIGH...I'M KINDA SICK OF ALL THE CONSTRUCTION AT SCHOOL.
I'M SURPRISED, LEE. YOU NEVER COMPLAIN!
PLUS, ALL THIS CONSTRUCTION'S A GOOD CHANCE TO TRAIN! WE CAN WORK...
ON STRENGTH!
ON AGILITY!
ON FLEXIBILITY AND BALANCE!
BLOM
ON CAMOUFLAGE?

Silence Is Golden

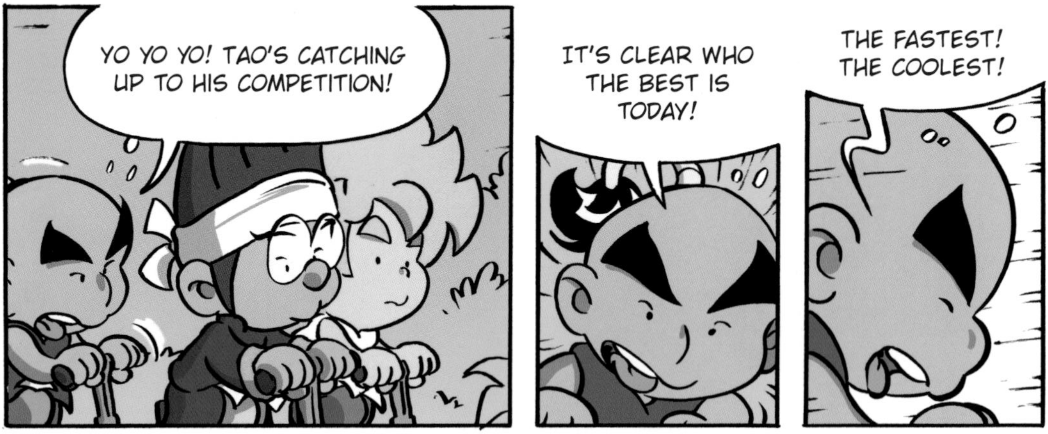
YO YO YO! TAO'S CATCHING UP TO HIS COMPETITION!
IT'S CLEAR WHO THE BEST IS TODAY!
THE FASTEST! THE COOLEST!

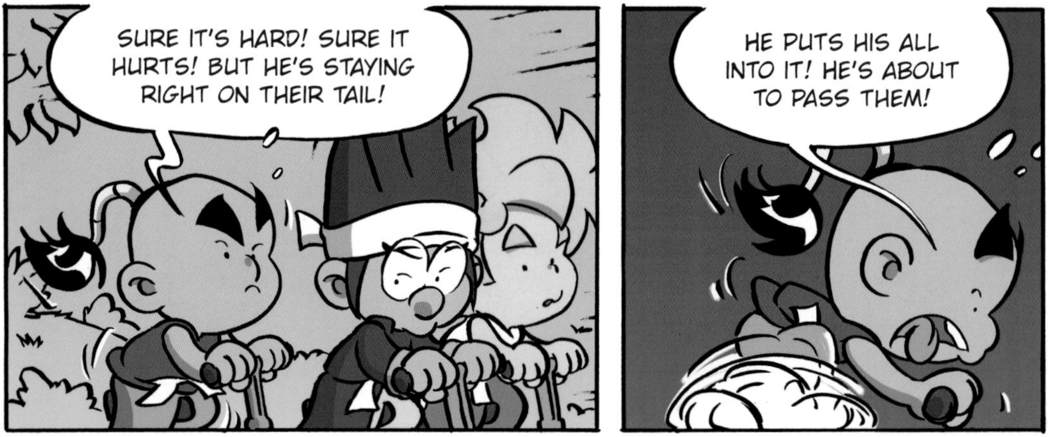
SURE IT'S HARD! SURE IT HURTS! BUT HE'S STAYING RIGHT ON THEIR TAIL!
HE PUTS HIS ALL INTO IT! HE'S ABOUT TO PASS THEM!

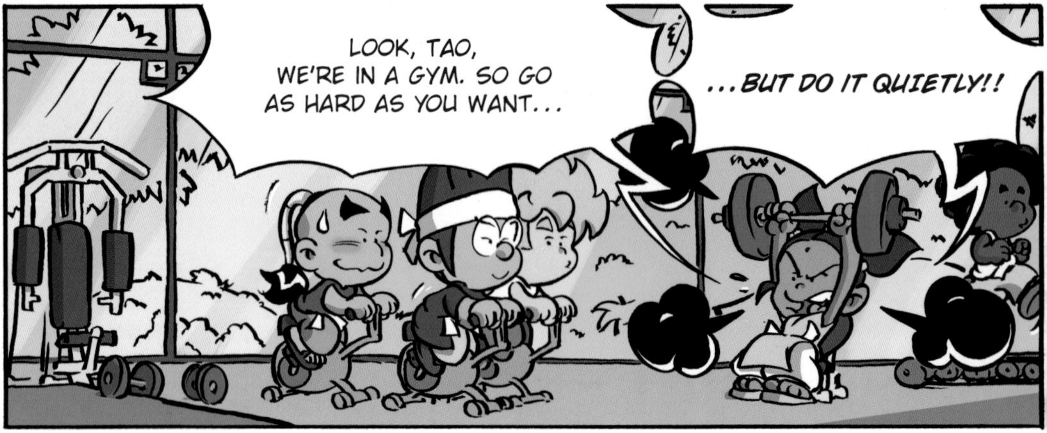
LOOK, TAO, WE'RE IN A GYM. SO GO AS HARD AS YOU WANT...
...BUT DO IT QUIETLY!!

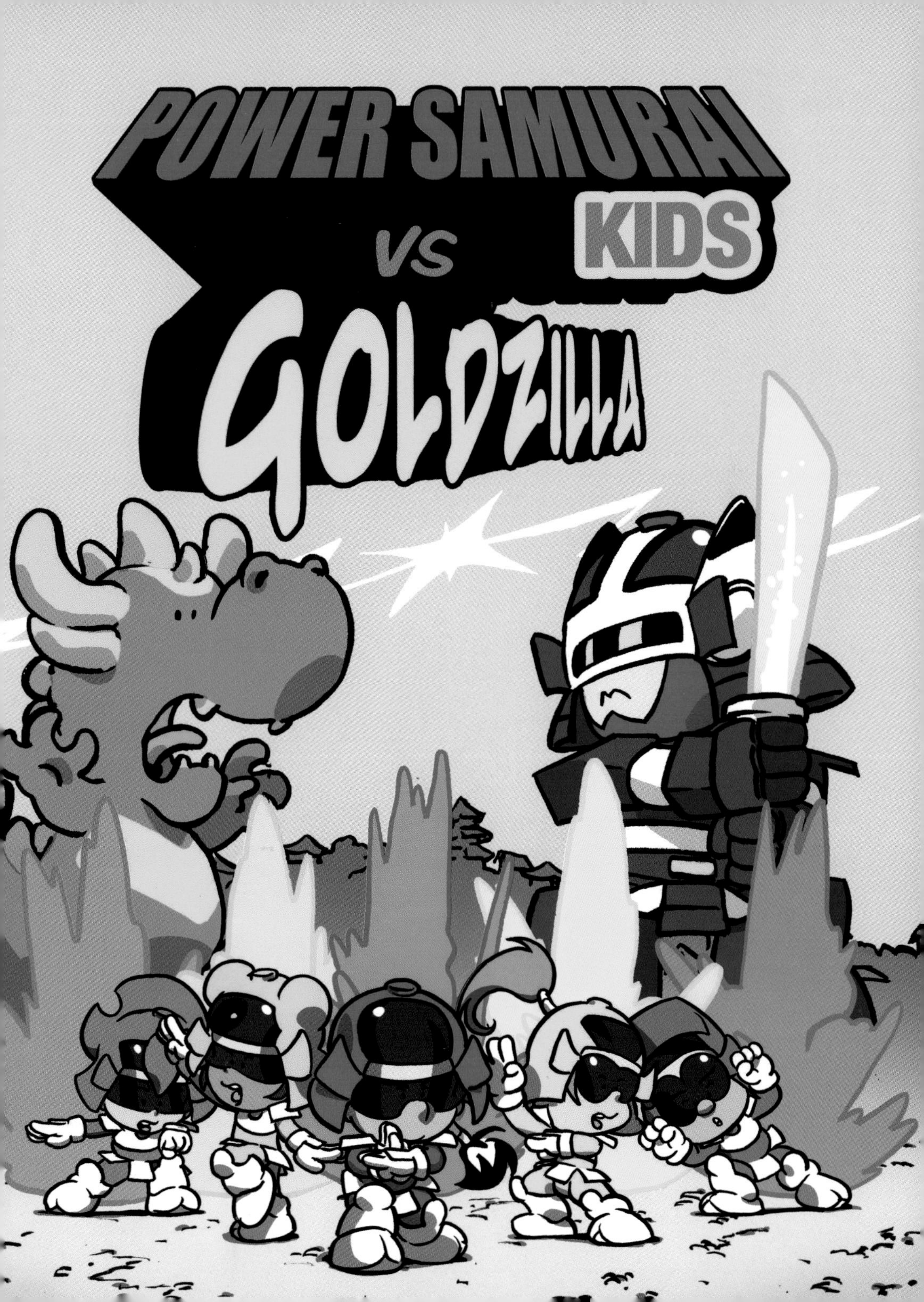
POWER SAMURAI KIDS
VS
GOLDZILLA

A Sixth Sense Shows the Way

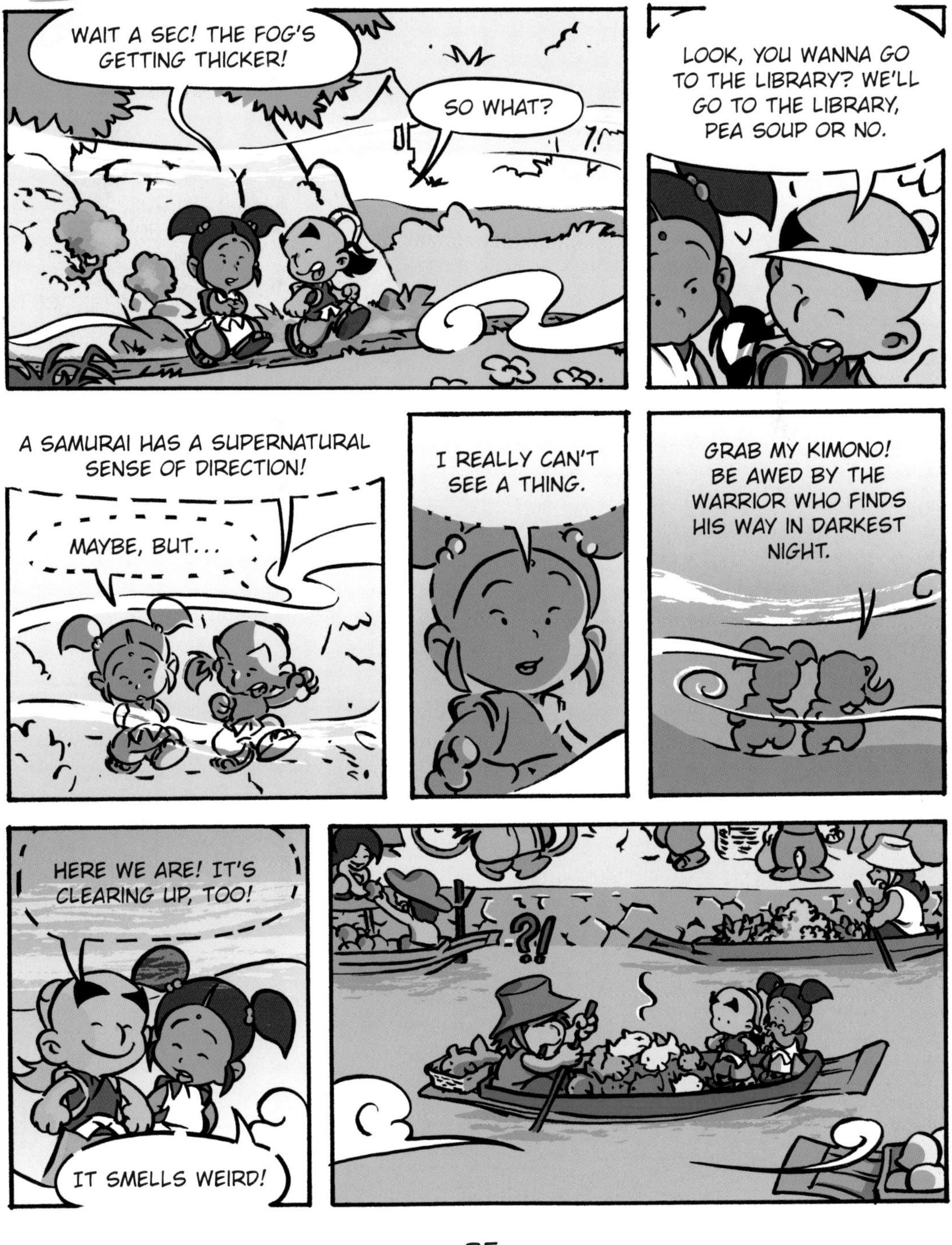
WAIT A SEC! THE FOG'S GETTING THICKER!
SO WHAT?
LOOK, YOU WANNA GO TO THE LIBRARY? WE'LL GO TO THE LIBRARY, PEA SOUP OR NO.
A SAMURAI HAS A SUPERNATURAL SENSE OF DIRECTION!
MAYBE, BUT...
I REALLY CAN'T SEE A THING.
GRAB MY KIMONO! BE AWED BY THE WARRIOR WHO FINDS HIS WAY IN DARKEST NIGHT.
HERE WE ARE! IT'S CLEARING UP, TOO!
IT SMELLS WEIRD!
?!

A Little Grasshopper Sure Can Be Loud

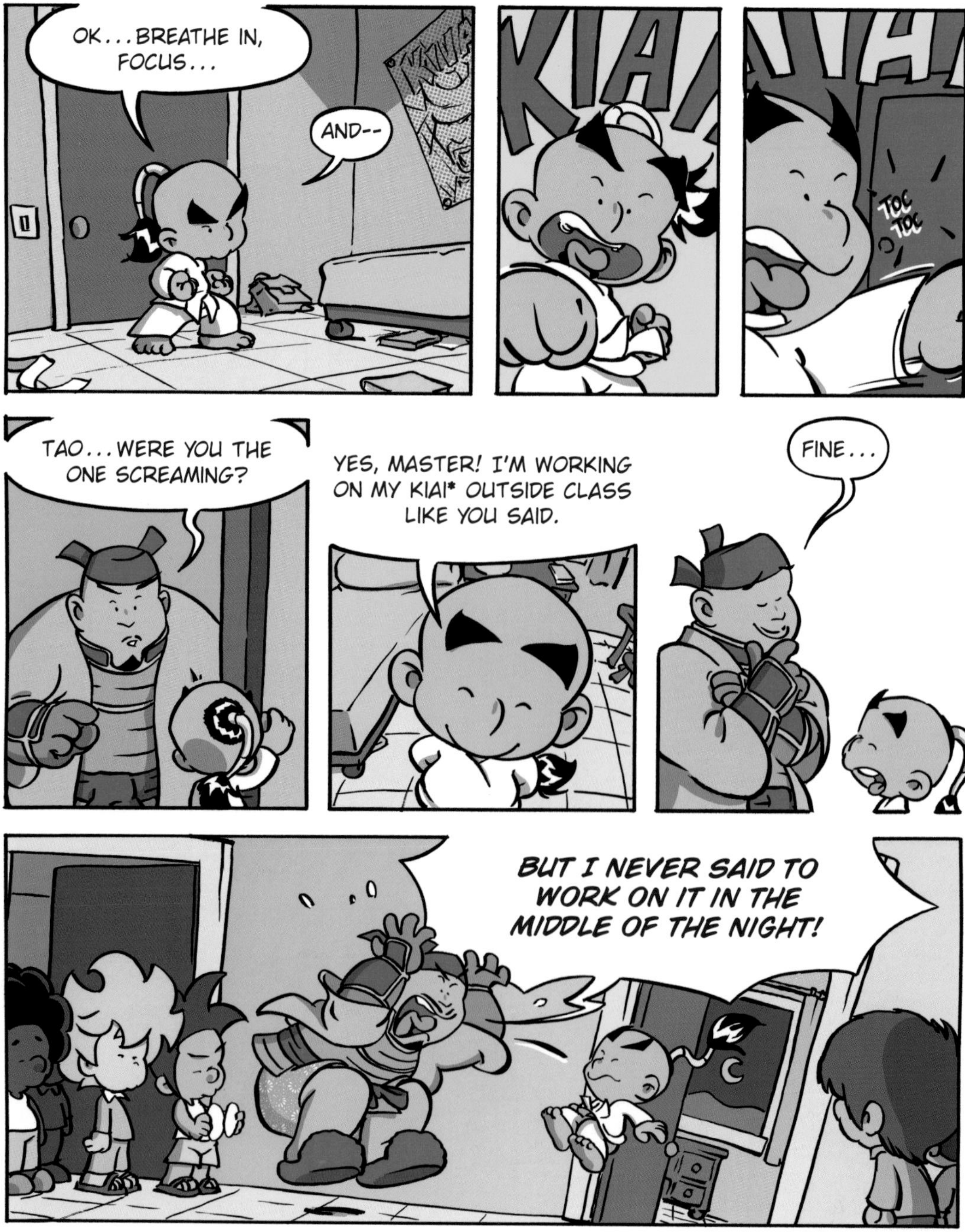
OK...BREATHE IN, FOCUS...
AND--
KIAIAAAAH
TOC TOC
TAO...WERE YOU THE ONE SCREAMING?
YES, MASTER! I'M WORKING ON MY KIAI* OUTSIDE CLASS LIKE YOU SAID.
FINE...
BUT I NEVER SAID TO WORK ON IT IN THE MIDDLE OF THE NIGHT!

*KIAI: A SHORT YELL MADE BY MARTIAL ARTISTS BEFORE, DURING, OR AFTER A MOVE

Silent but Deadly

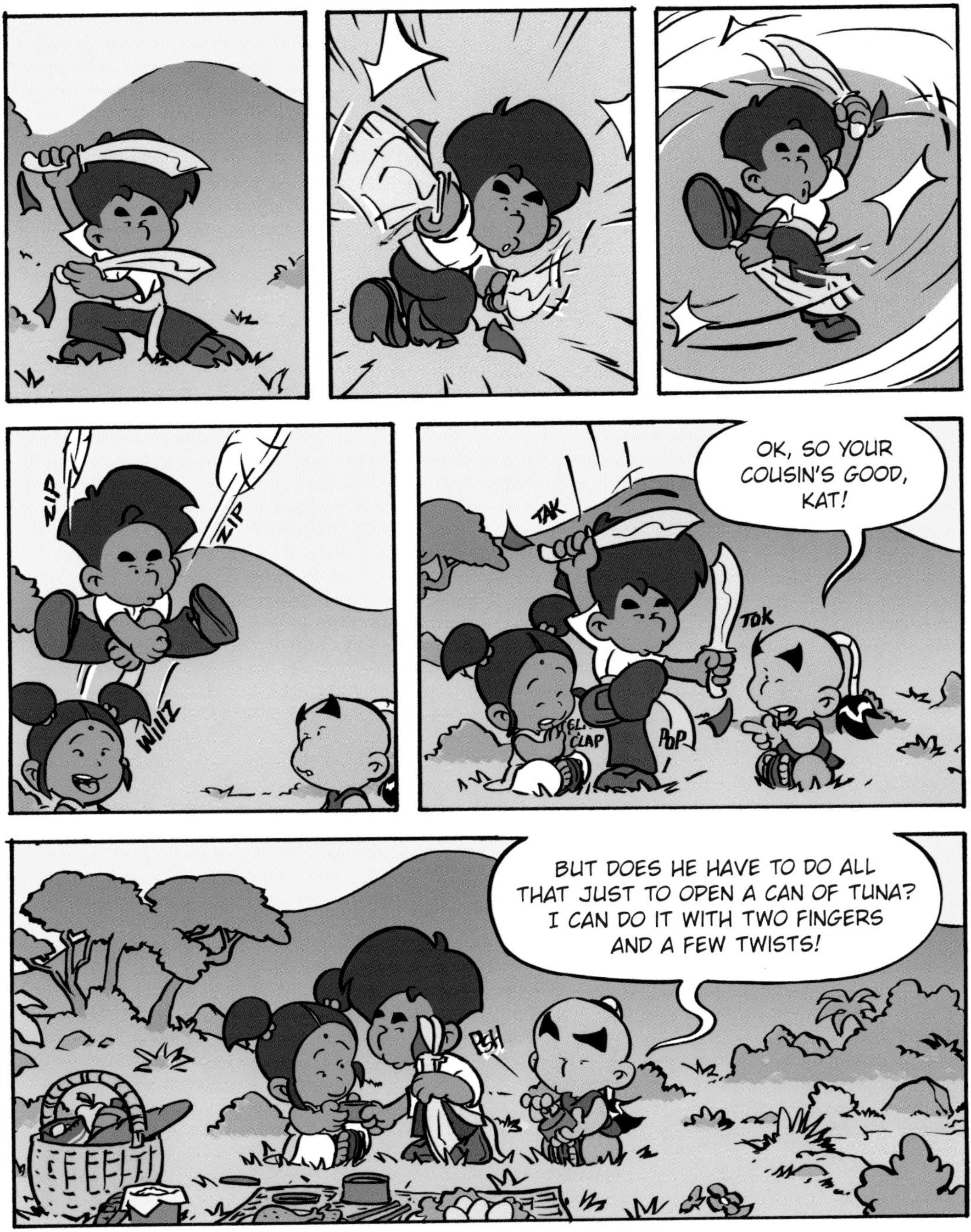
ZIP
ZIP
OK, SO YOUR COUSIN'S GOOD, KAT!
TAK
TOK
CLAP
POP!
BUT DOES HE HAVE TO DO ALL THAT JUST TO OPEN A CAN OF TUNA? I CAN DO IT WITH TWO FINGERS AND A FEW TWISTS!
PSH

The Path to Sharing Is Long and Slippery

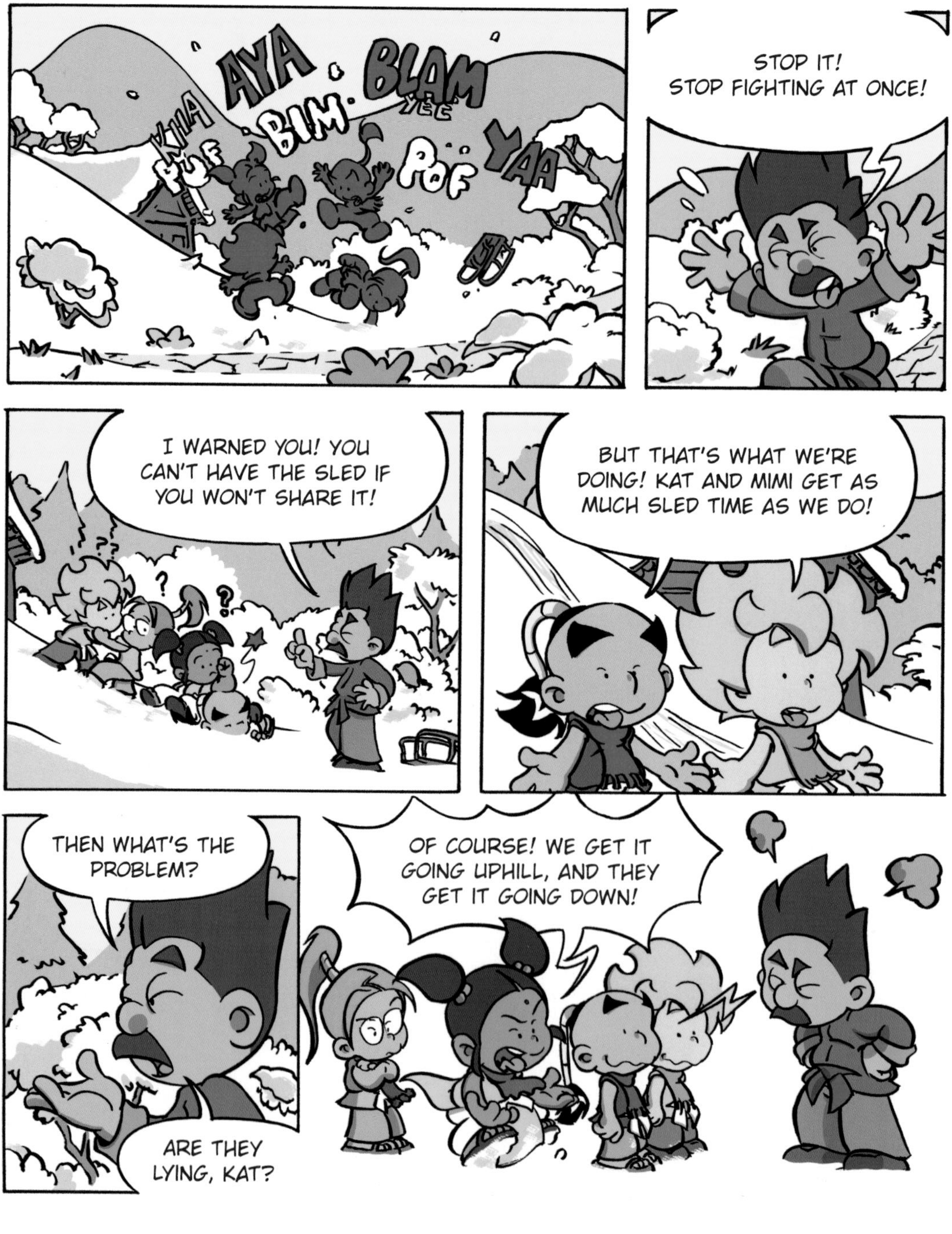
AYA
BLAM
BIM
YEE
POF
POF
YAA
STOP IT!
STOP FIGHTING AT ONCE!
I WARNED YOU! YOU CAN'T HAVE THE SLED IF YOU WON'T SHARE IT!
BUT THAT'S WHAT WE'RE DOING! KAT AND MIMI GET AS MUCH SLED TIME AS WE DO!
THEN WHAT'S THE PROBLEM?
ARE THEY LYING, KAT?
OF COURSE! WE GET IT GOING UPHILL, AND THEY GET IT GOING DOWN!

The Karate Woodsman Works Hard at Christmas

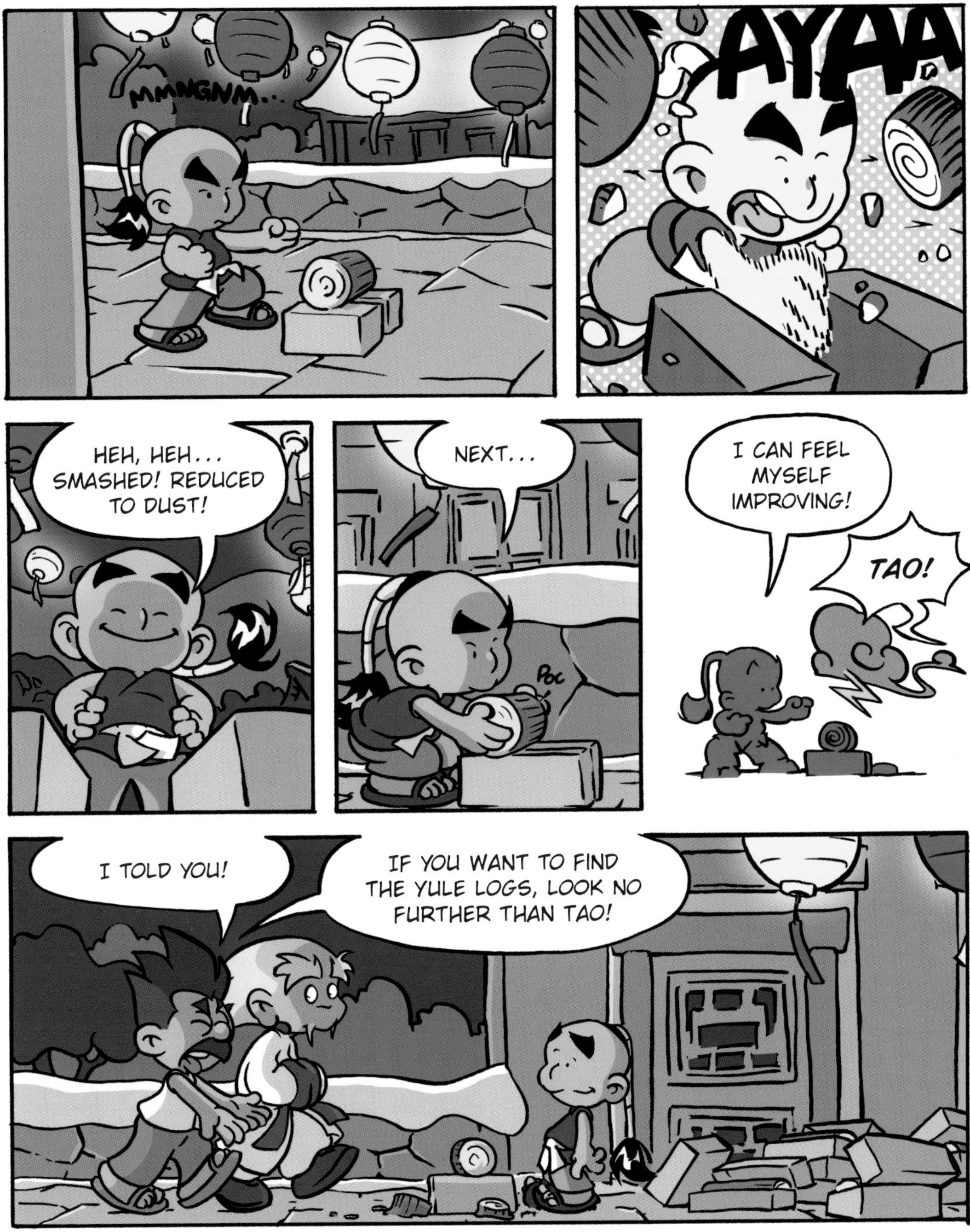
MMNGNM...
AYAA
HEH, HEH... SMASHED! REDUCED TO DUST!
NEXT...
POC
I CAN FEEL MYSELF IMPROVING!
TAO!
I TOLD YOU!
IF YOU WANT TO FIND THE YULE LOGS, LOOK NO FURTHER THAN TAO!

Snow Days

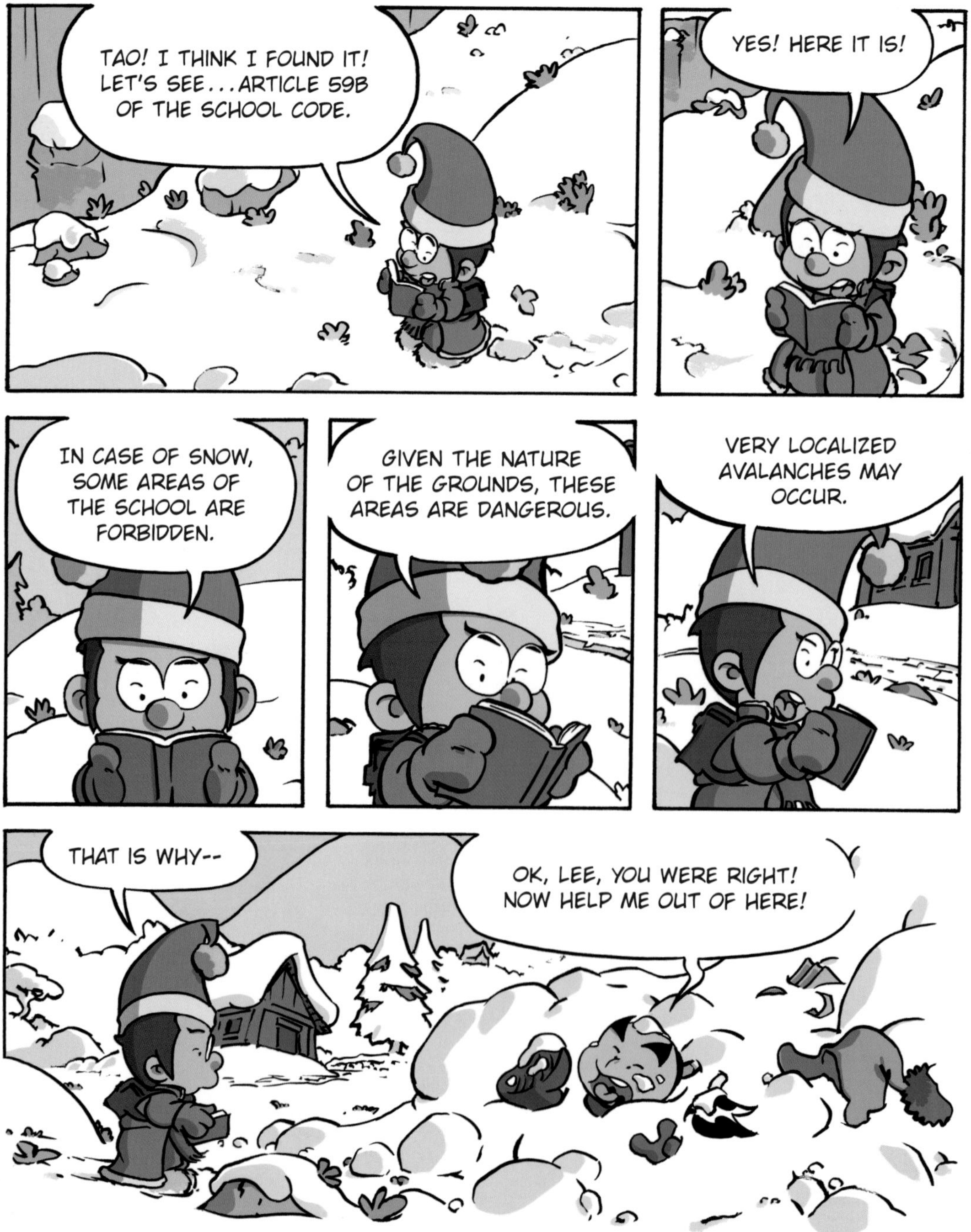

TAO! I THINK I FOUND IT! LET'S SEE... ARTICLE 59B OF THE SCHOOL CODE.
YES! HERE IT IS!
IN CASE OF SNOW, SOME AREAS OF THE SCHOOL ARE FORBIDDEN.
GIVEN THE NATURE OF THE GROUNDS, THESE AREAS ARE DANGEROUS.
VERY LOCALIZED AVALANCHES MAY OCCUR.
THAT IS WHY--
OK, LEE, YOU WERE RIGHT! NOW HELP ME OUT OF HERE!

Mirror, Mirror on the Wall

WELL, THIS TIME THERE'S NO DOUBTING IT!

TAO IS THE CHAMPION OF THE WORLD!

TCHACK

THE BIGGEST! THE STRONGEST! THE HANDSOMEST!

SLURP SLURP

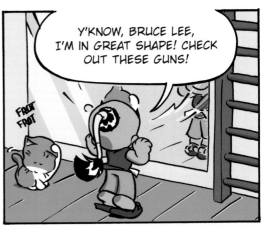

Y'KNOW, BRUCE LEE, I'M IN GREAT SHAPE! CHECK OUT THESE GUNS!

FROT FROT

...

FF FF FF FF FF FF FF

SIGH...SOME GUYS JUST LIVE TO SHOW OFF...

31

Fetching Fletching

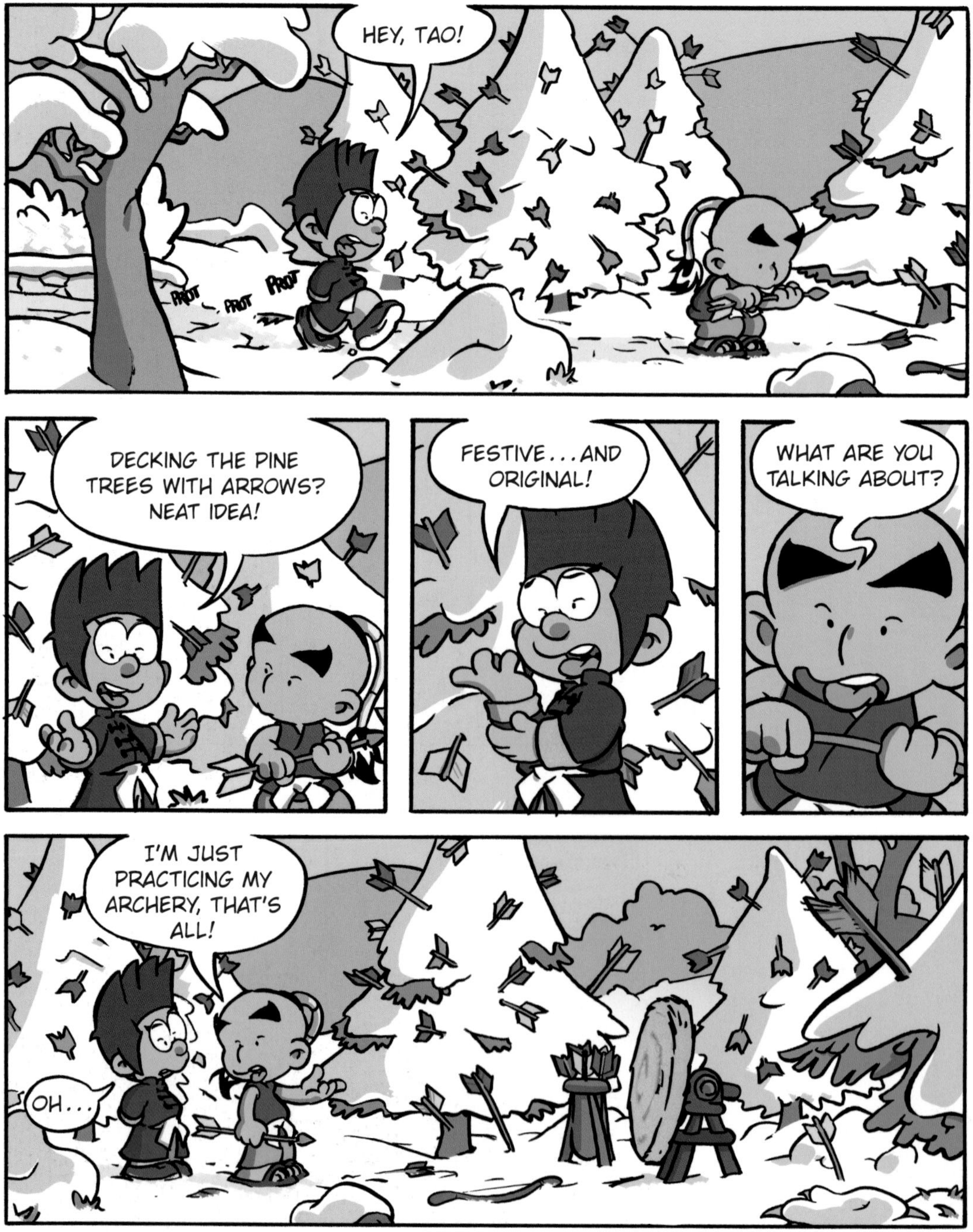

HEY, TAO!
PROT PROT PROT
DECKING THE PINE TREES WITH ARROWS? NEAT IDEA!
FESTIVE....AND ORIGINAL!
WHAT ARE YOU TALKING ABOUT?
I'M JUST PRACTICING MY ARCHERY, THAT'S ALL!
OH...

A Samurai's Training Never Stops

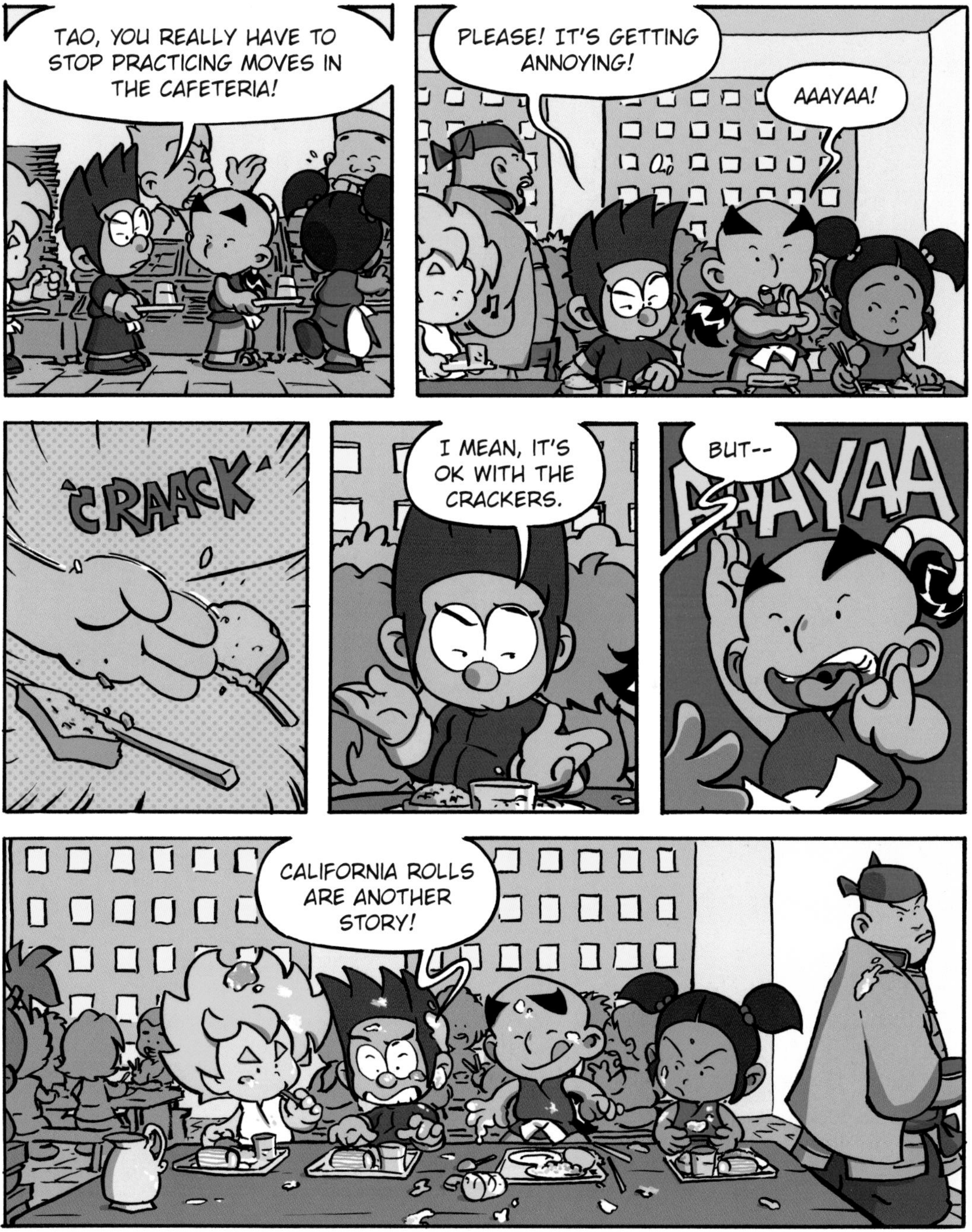

TAO, YOU REALLY HAVE TO STOP PRACTICING MOVES IN THE CAFETERIA!
PLEASE! IT'S GETTING ANNOYING!
AAAYAA!
CRAACK
I MEAN, IT'S OK WITH THE CRACKERS.
BUT--
AAAYAA
CALIFORNIA ROLLS ARE ANOTHER STORY!

Still Life or Still Alive?

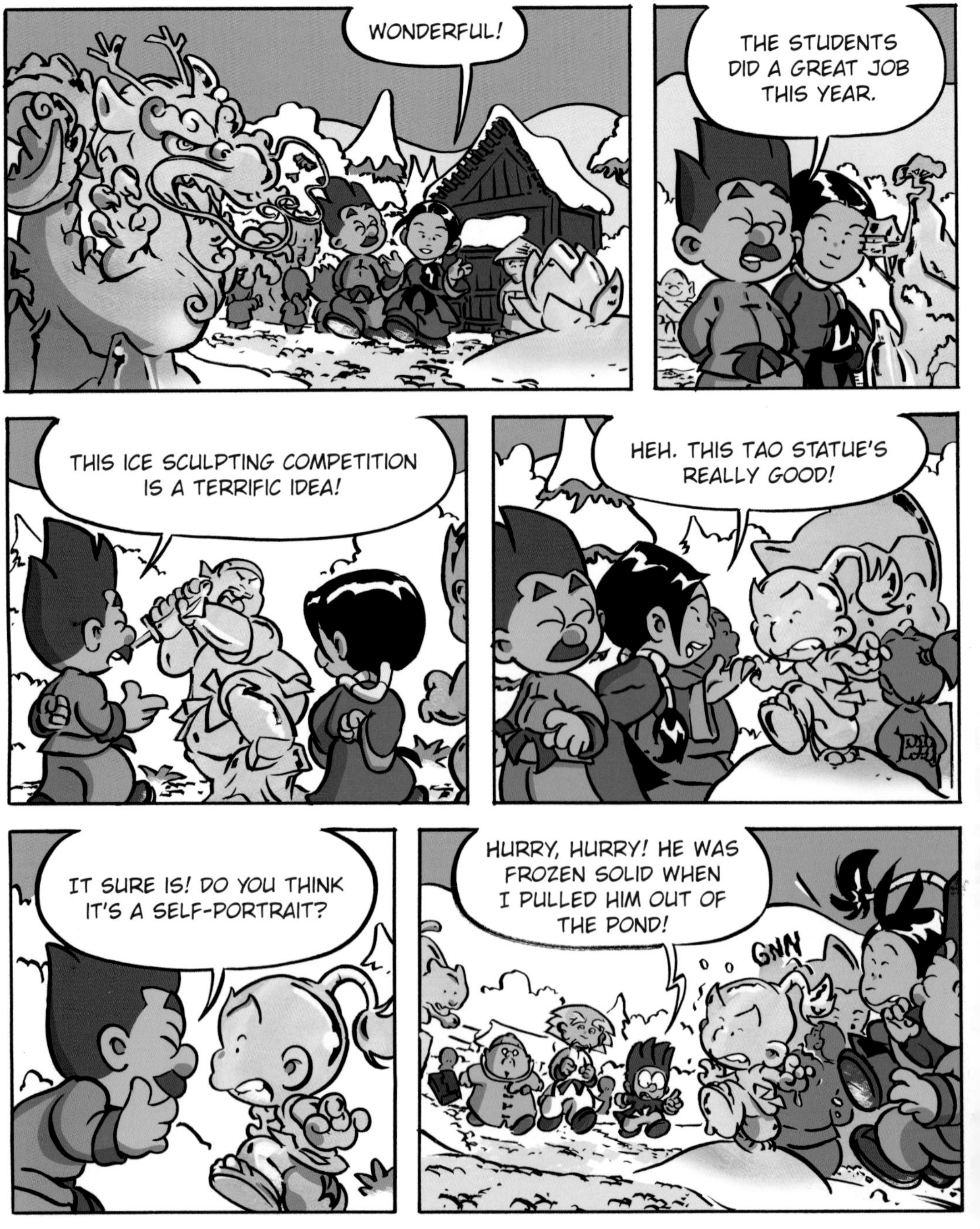
WONDERFUL!
THE STUDENTS DID A GREAT JOB THIS YEAR.
THIS ICE SCULPTING COMPETITION IS A TERRIFIC IDEA!
HEH. THIS TAO STATUE'S REALLY GOOD!
IT SURE IS! DO YOU THINK IT'S A SELF-PORTRAIT?
HURRY, HURRY! HE WAS FROZEN SOLID WHEN I PULLED HIM OUT OF THE POND!
GNN

A Loving Cry

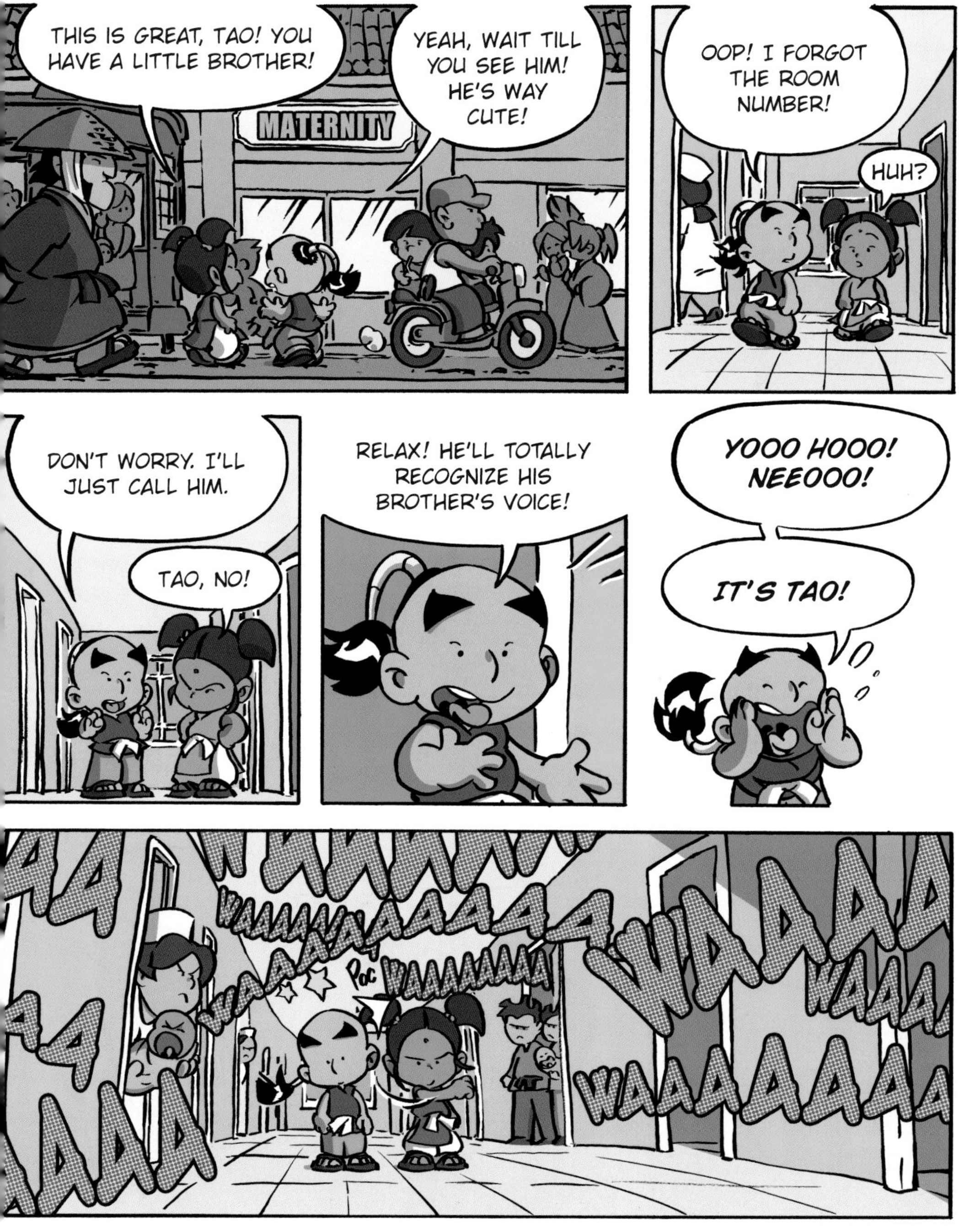
THIS IS GREAT, TAO! YOU HAVE A LITTLE BROTHER!
YEAH, WAIT TILL YOU SEE HIM! HE'S WAY CUTE!
MATERNITY
OOP! I FORGOT THE ROOM NUMBER!
HUH?
DON'T WORRY. I'LL JUST CALL HIM.
TAO, NO!
RELAX! HE'LL TOTALLY RECOGNIZE HIS BROTHER'S VOICE!
YOOO HOOO! NEEOOO!
IT'S TAO!
WAAAAAAAAA
POC
WAAAAAAAA
WAAAAAAAA

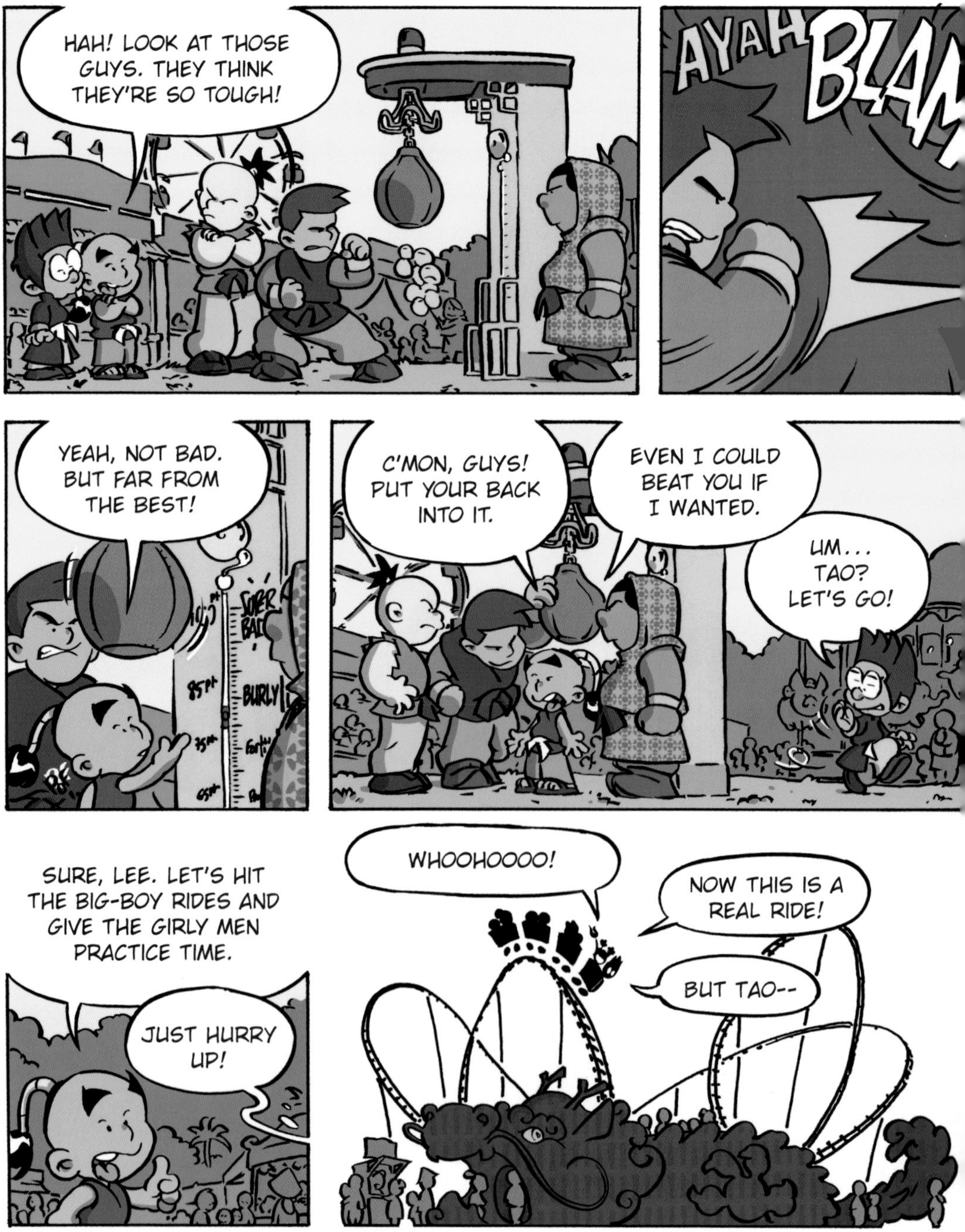
HAH! LOOK AT THOSE GUYS. THEY THINK THEY'RE SO TOUGH!
AYAH
BLAM
YEAH, NOT BAD. BUT FAR FROM THE BEST!
C'MON, GUYS! PUT YOUR BACK INTO IT.
EVEN I COULD BEAT YOU IF I WANTED.
UM... TAO? LET'S GO!
SURE, LEE. LET'S HIT THE BIG-BOY RIDES AND GIVE THE GIRLY MEN PRACTICE TIME.
JUST HURRY UP!
WHOOHOOOO!
NOW THIS IS A REAL RIDE!
BUT TAO--

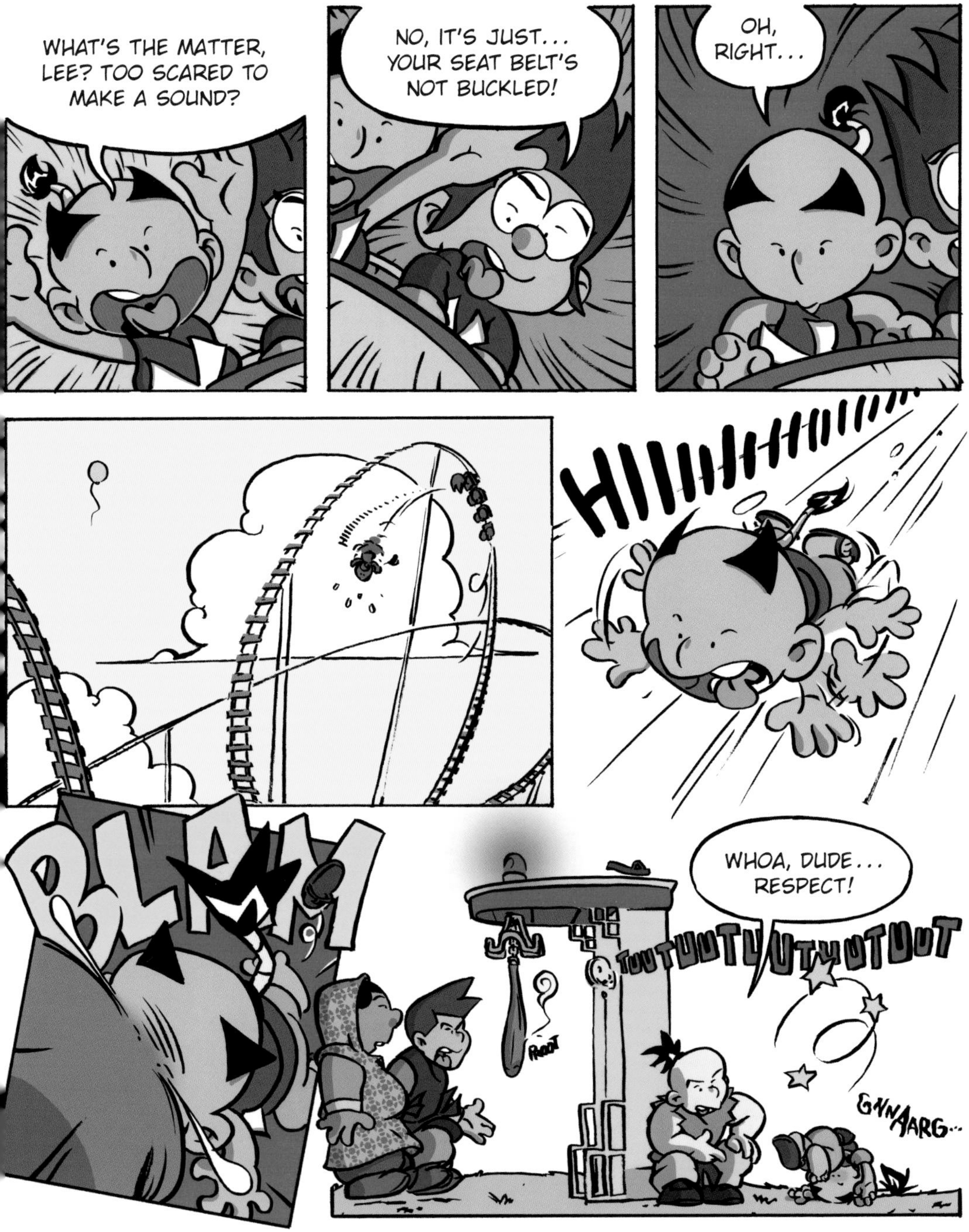

WHAT'S THE MATTER, LEE? TOO SCARED TO MAKE A SOUND?
NO, IT'S JUST... YOUR SEAT BELT'S NOT BUCKLED!
OH, RIGHT...
HIIIIIIIIIII...
WHOA, DUDE... RESPECT!
TUUTUUTUUTUUTUUT
GNNAARG...

A Samurai's Modest Gifts

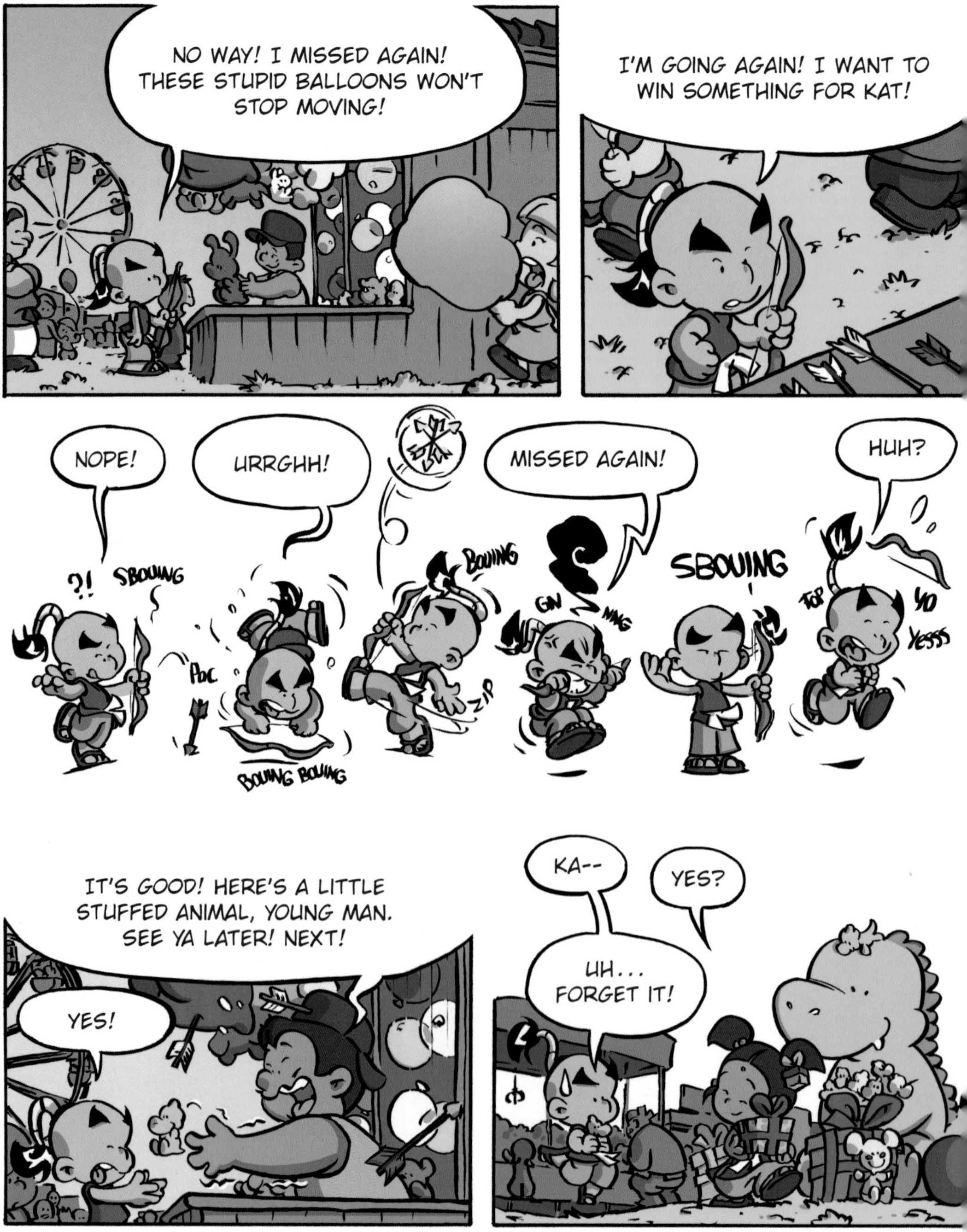

NO WAY! I MISSED AGAIN! THESE STUPID BALLOONS WON'T STOP MOVING!
I'M GOING AGAIN! I WANT TO WIN SOMETHING FOR KAT!
NOPE!
?!
SBOUING
POC
URRGHH!
BOUING BOUING
BOUING
ZIP
MISSED AGAIN!
GN
NAG
SBOUING
HUH?
TOP
YO
YESSS
IT'S GOOD! HERE'S A LITTLE STUFFED ANIMAL, YOUNG MAN. SEE YA LATER! NEXT!
YES!
KA--
YES?
UH... FORGET IT!

Book Learning Is Easy on the Ear

. . . what matters most in a kata is spirit. Rhythm; stances, whether low, high . . .

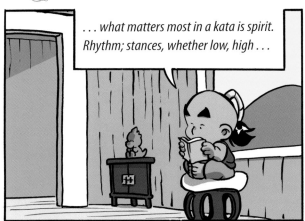

. . . or sustained; and all our inner human qualities. Also keenness of vision, mental focus from beginning to end, and total physical concentration reinforcing . . . *

WHOA! VERY IMPRESSIVE, TAO!

MY SON, STUDYING HIS BOOKS! WHAT A RARE SIGHT!

WEEELL . . .

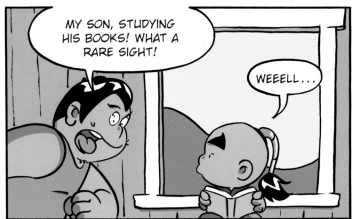

THIS WAS THE ONLY THING THAT PUT NEO TO SLEEP. WHEN I STOP READING, HE CRIES!

ZZZ ZZZ

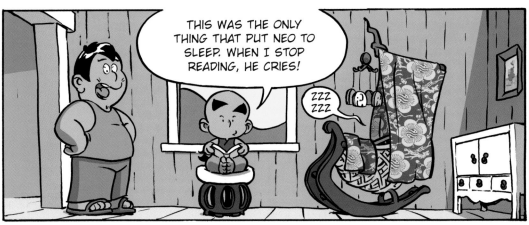

*HENRY PLÉE, KARATE BLACK BELT

A Dragon in Love Sometimes Breathes Fire

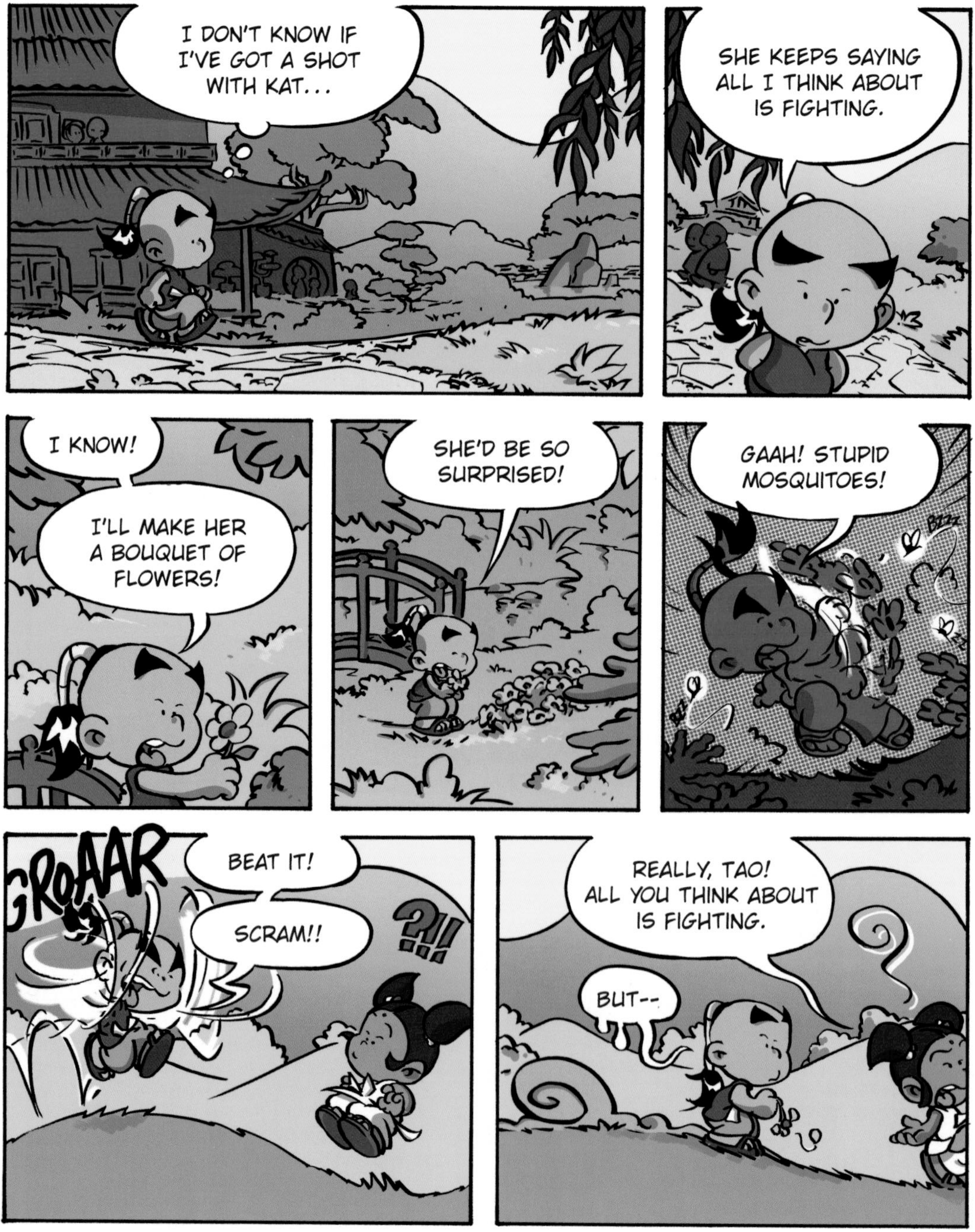

I DON'T KNOW IF I'VE GOT A SHOT WITH KAT...
SHE KEEPS SAYING ALL I THINK ABOUT IS FIGHTING.
I KNOW!
I'LL MAKE HER A BOUQUET OF FLOWERS!
SHE'D BE SO SURPRISED!
GAAH! STUPID MOSQUITOES!
GROAAR
BEAT IT!
SCRAM!!
?!!
REALLY, TAO! ALL YOU THINK ABOUT IS FIGHTING.
BUT--

Flying Off the Handle

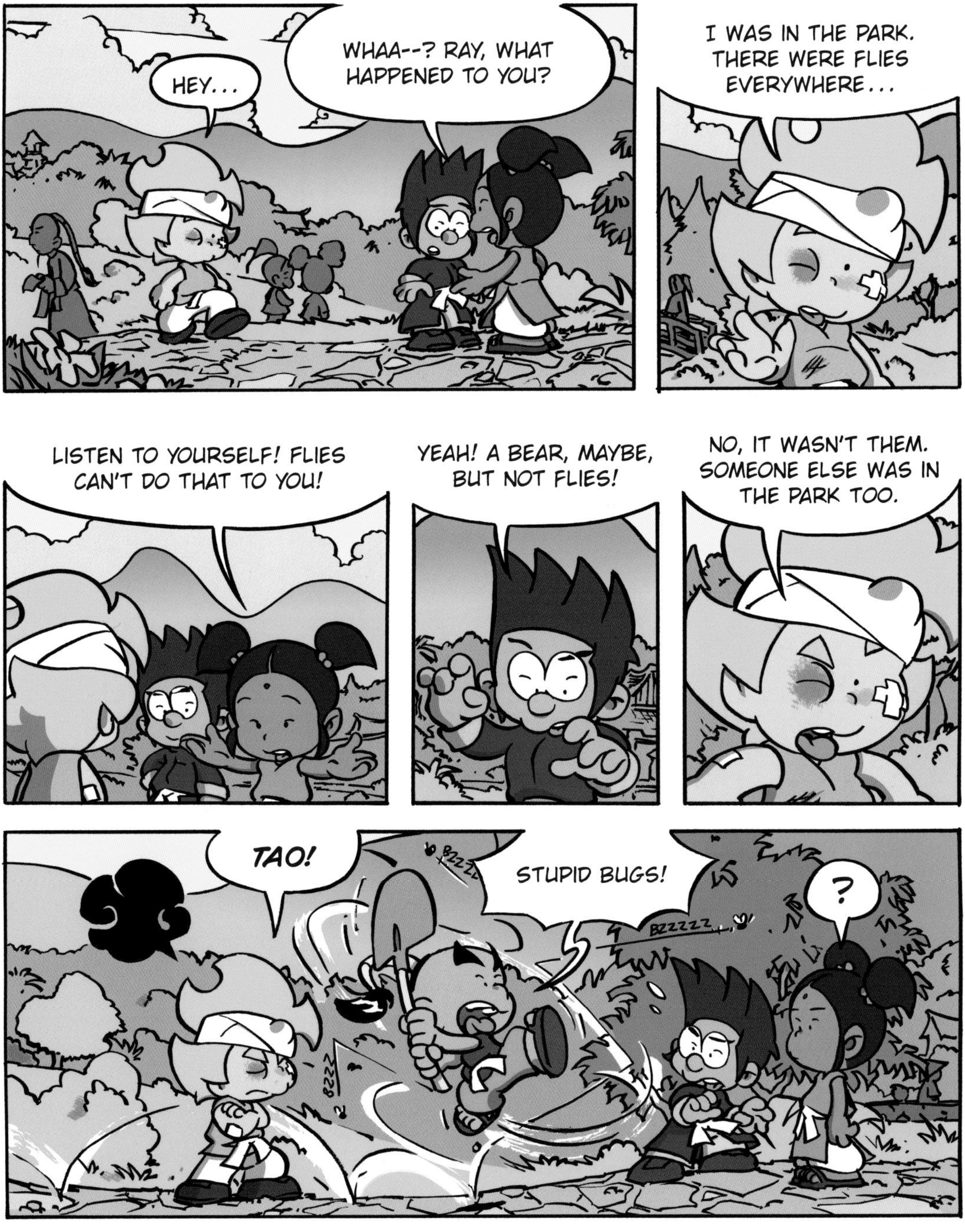
HEY...
WHAA--? RAY, WHAT HAPPENED TO YOU?
I WAS IN THE PARK. THERE WERE FLIES EVERYWHERE...
LISTEN TO YOURSELF! FLIES CAN'T DO THAT TO YOU!
YEAH! A BEAR, MAYBE, BUT NOT FLIES!
NO, IT WASN'T THEM. SOMEONE ELSE WAS IN THE PARK TOO.
TAO!
STUPID BUGS!
BZZZZZ
?

Grasshopper, Listen to Your Elders

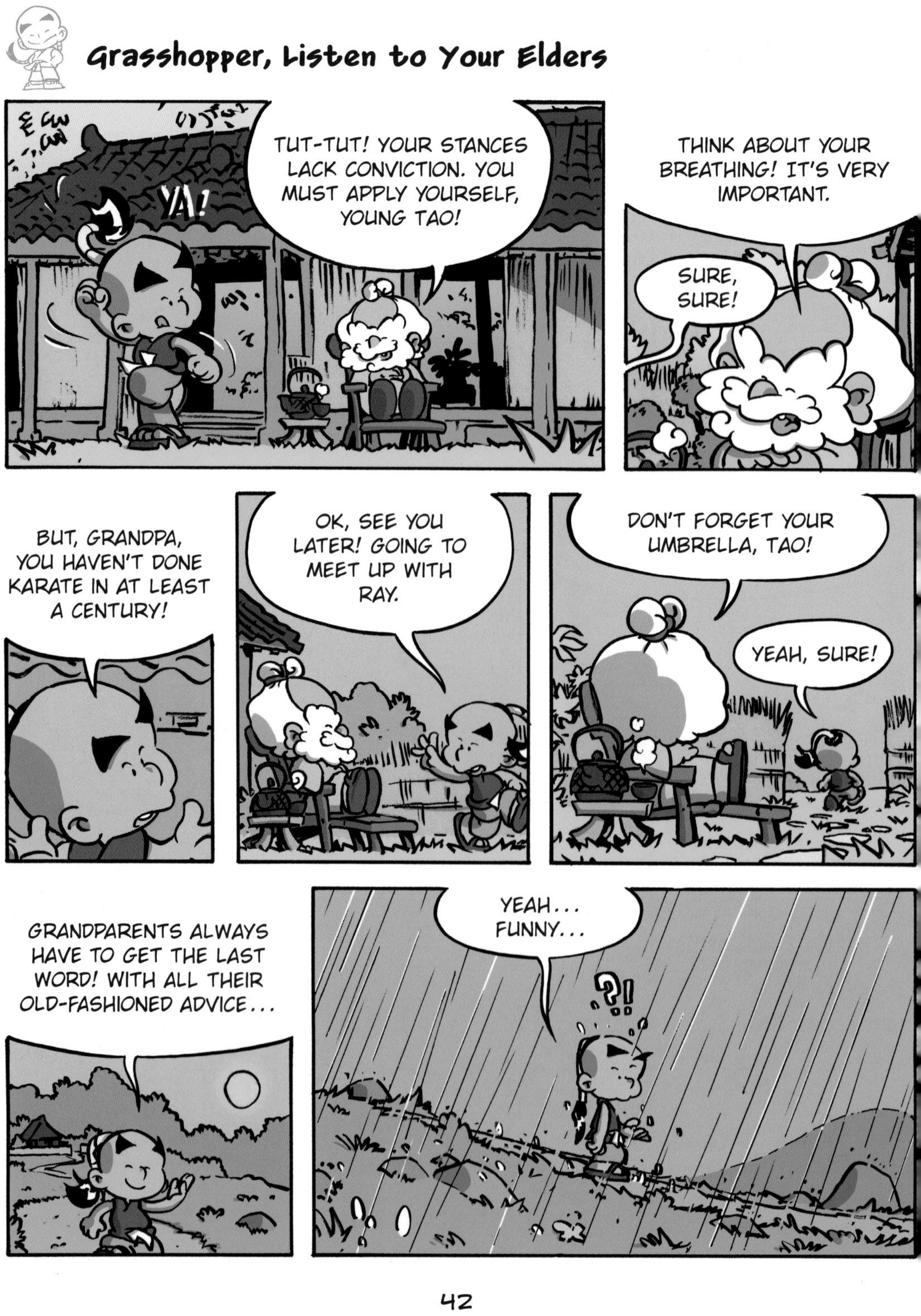
YA!
TUT-TUT! YOUR STANCES LACK CONVICTION. YOU MUST APPLY YOURSELF, YOUNG TAO!
THINK ABOUT YOUR BREATHING! IT'S VERY IMPORTANT.
SURE, SURE!
BUT, GRANDPA, YOU HAVEN'T DONE KARATE IN AT LEAST A CENTURY!
OK, SEE YOU LATER! GOING TO MEET UP WITH RAY.
DON'T FORGET YOUR UMBRELLA, TAO!
YEAH, SURE!
GRANDPARENTS ALWAYS HAVE TO GET THE LAST WORD! WITH ALL THEIR OLD-FASHIONED ADVICE...
YEAH... FUNNY...
?!

The True Test of a Samurai

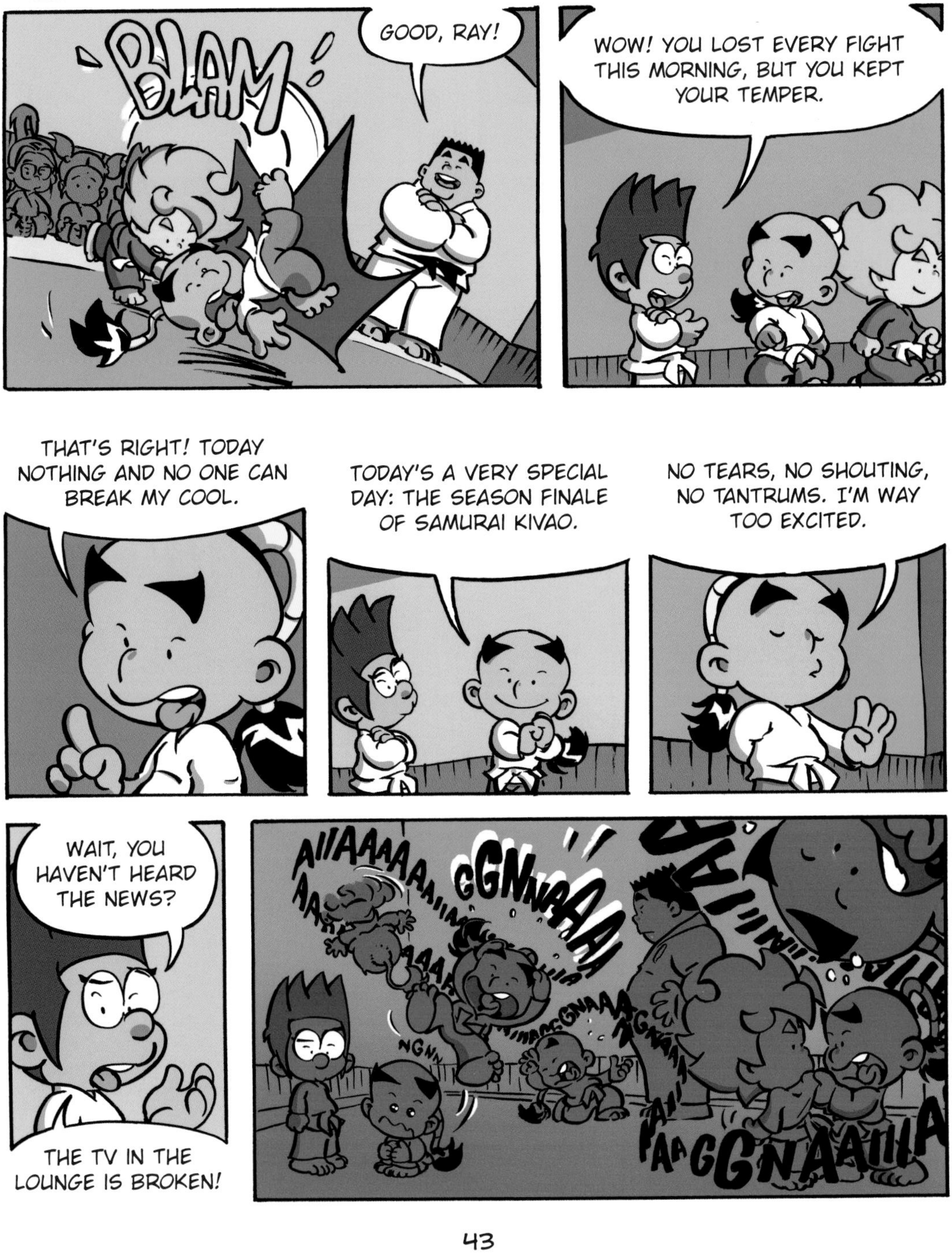
BLAM
GOOD, RAY!
WOW! YOU LOST EVERY FIGHT THIS MORNING, BUT YOU KEPT YOUR TEMPER.
THAT'S RIGHT! TODAY NOTHING AND NO ONE CAN BREAK MY COOL.
TODAY'S A VERY SPECIAL DAY: THE SEASON FINALE OF SAMURAI KIVAO.
NO TEARS, NO SHOUTING, NO TANTRUMS. I'M WAY TOO EXCITED.
WAIT, YOU HAVEN'T HEARD THE NEWS?
THE TV IN THE LOUNGE IS BROKEN!

Hunger Is a Powerful Motivator

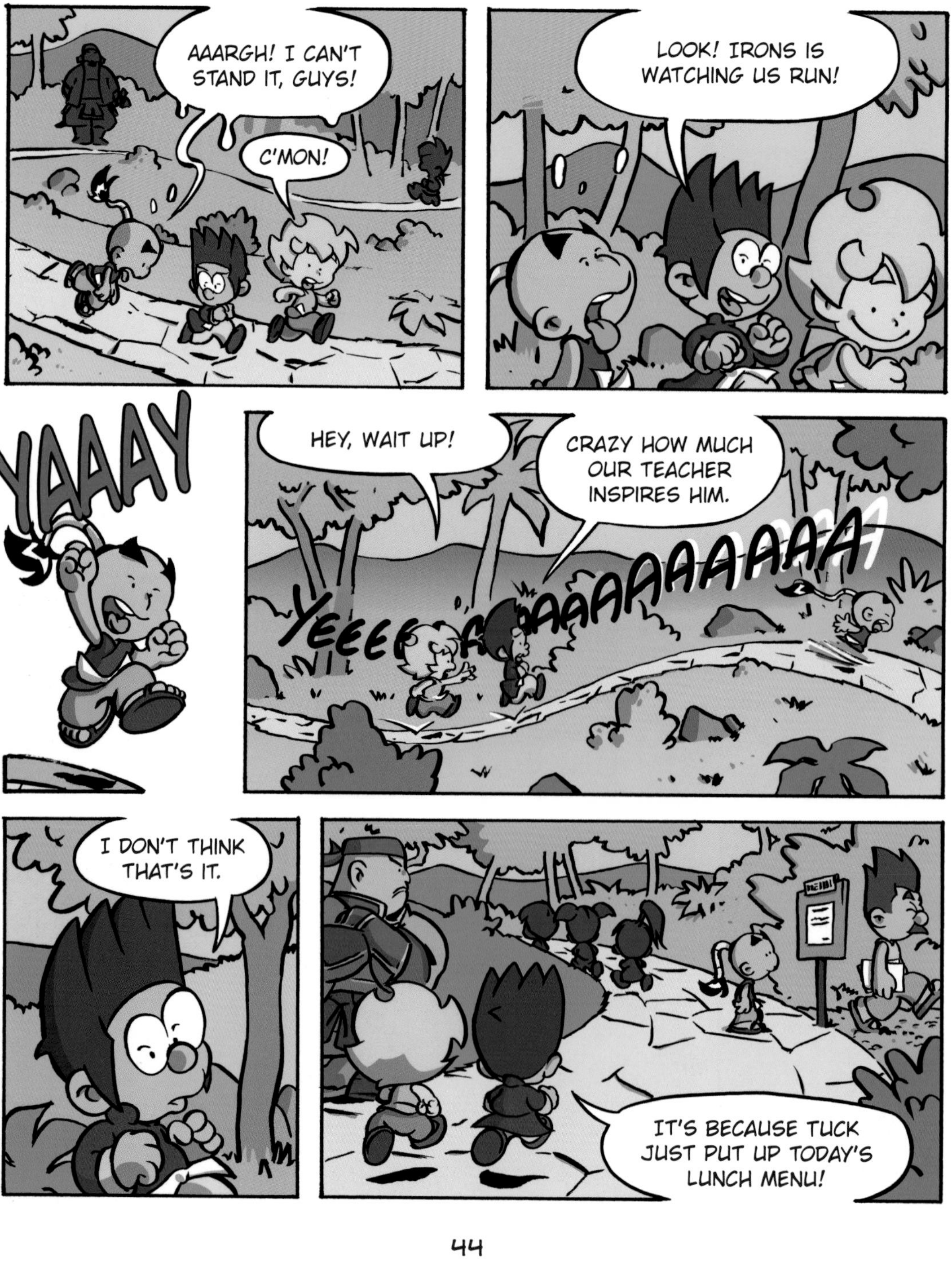

AAARGH! I CAN'T STAND IT, GUYS!
C'MON!
LOOK! IRONS IS WATCHING US RUN!
YAAAY
HEY, WAIT UP!
CRAZY HOW MUCH OUR TEACHER INSPIRES HIM.
YEEEEAAAAAAAAAAAA
I DON'T THINK THAT'S IT.
IT'S BECAUSE TUCK JUST PUT UP TODAY'S LUNCH MENU!

The Great Ninja Knows (Almost) No Fear

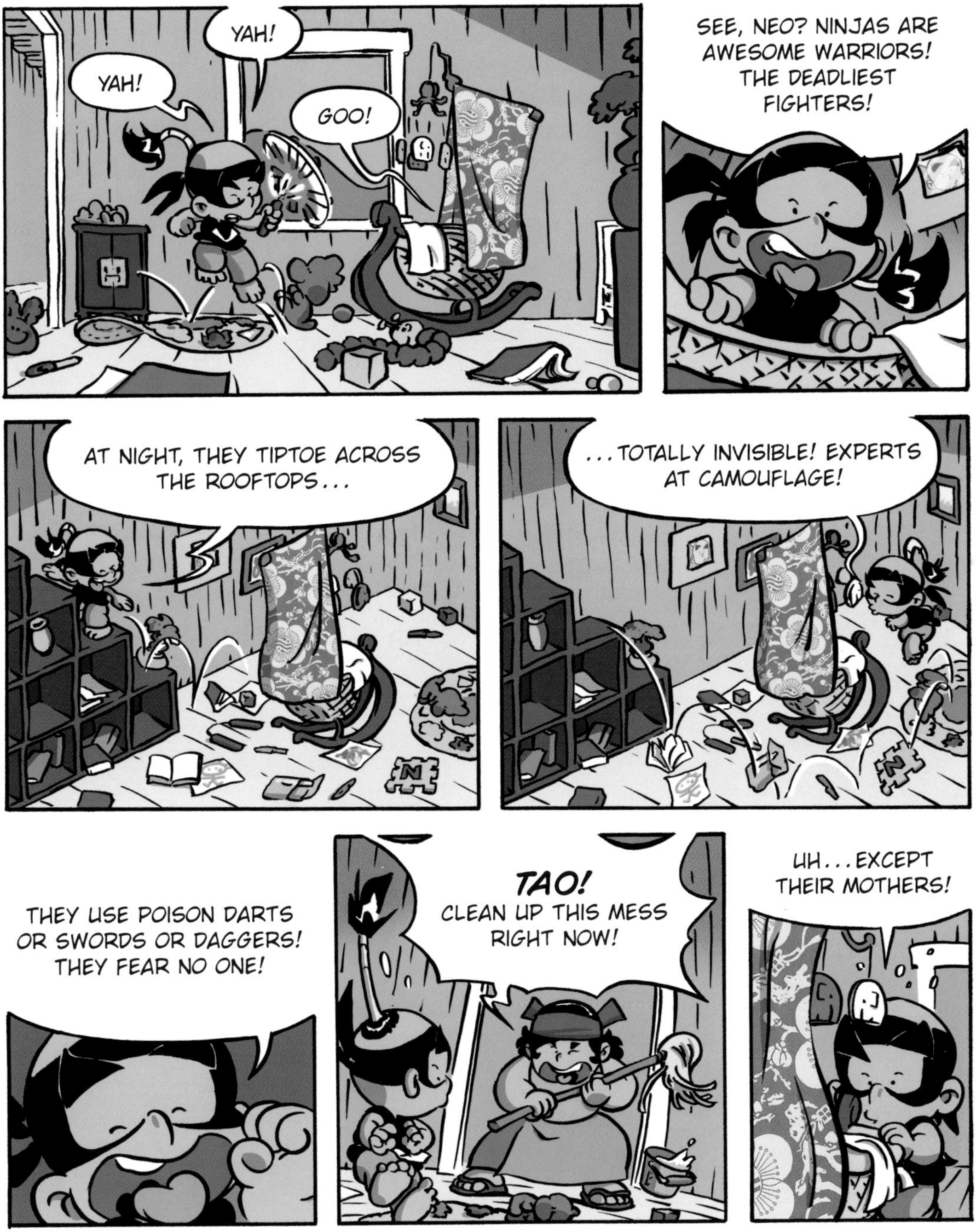
YAH!
YAH!
GOO!
SEE, NEO? NINJAS ARE AWESOME WARRIORS! THE DEADLIEST FIGHTERS!
AT NIGHT, THEY TIPTOE ACROSS THE ROOFTOPS...
...TOTALLY INVISIBLE! EXPERTS AT CAMOUFLAGE!
THEY USE POISON DARTS OR SWORDS OR DAGGERS! THEY FEAR NO ONE!
TAO! CLEAN UP THIS MESS RIGHT NOW!
UH...EXCEPT THEIR MOTHERS!

Lightning-Fast Reflexes

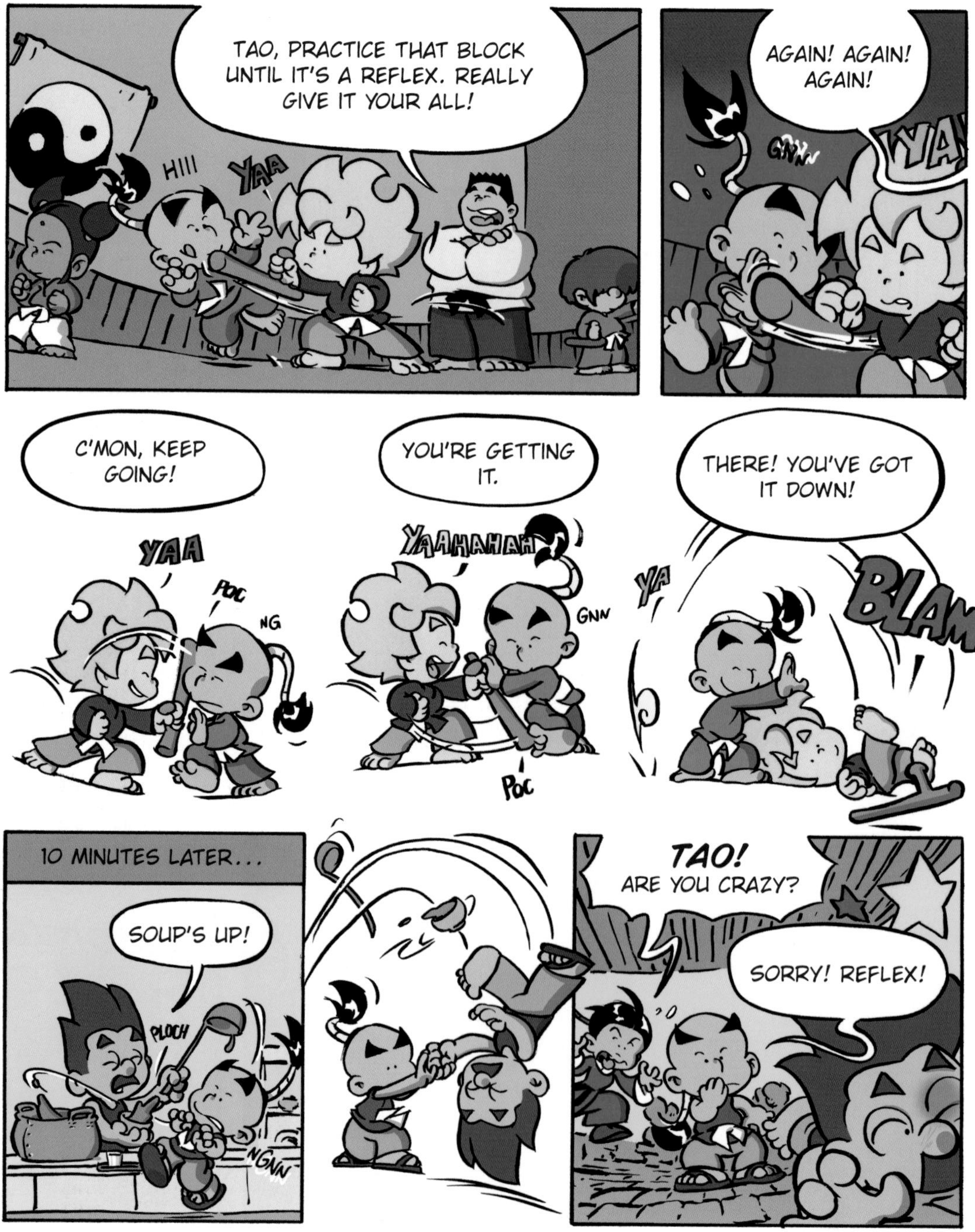
TAO, PRACTICE THAT BLOCK UNTIL IT'S A REFLEX. REALLY GIVE IT YOUR ALL!
HIII
YAA
AGAIN! AGAIN! AGAIN!
GNN
YAA
C'MON, KEEP GOING!
YAA
POC
NG
YOU'RE GETTING IT.
YAAHAHAH
GNN
POC
THERE! YOU'VE GOT IT DOWN!
YA
BLAM
10 MINUTES LATER...
SOUP'S UP!
PLOCH
NGNN
TAO!
ARE YOU CRAZY?
SORRY! REFLEX!

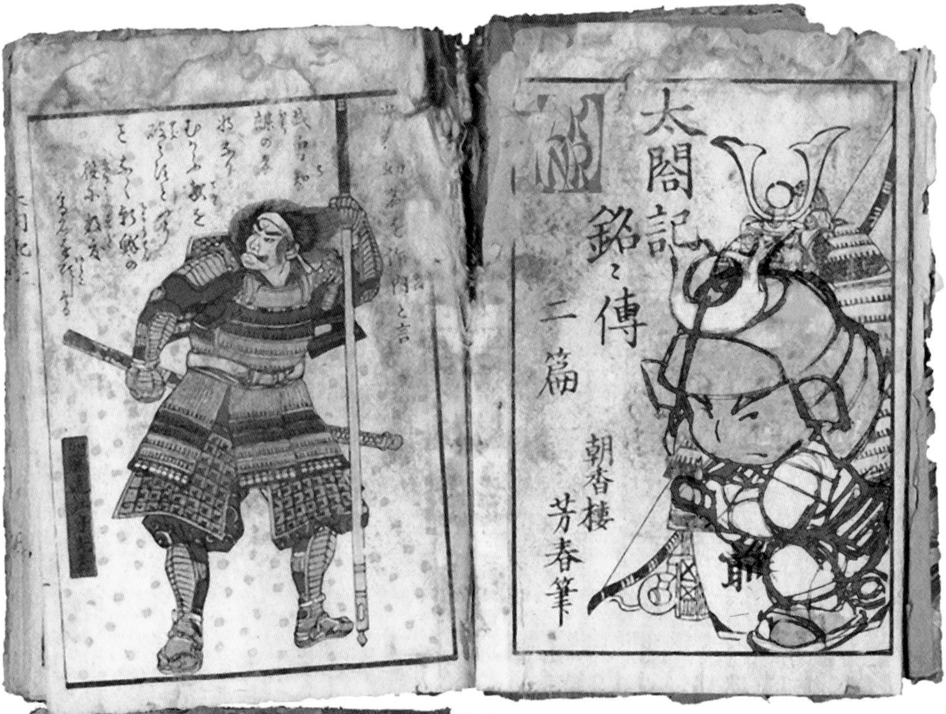
太閤記
銘々傳
二篇
朝香楼
芳春筆

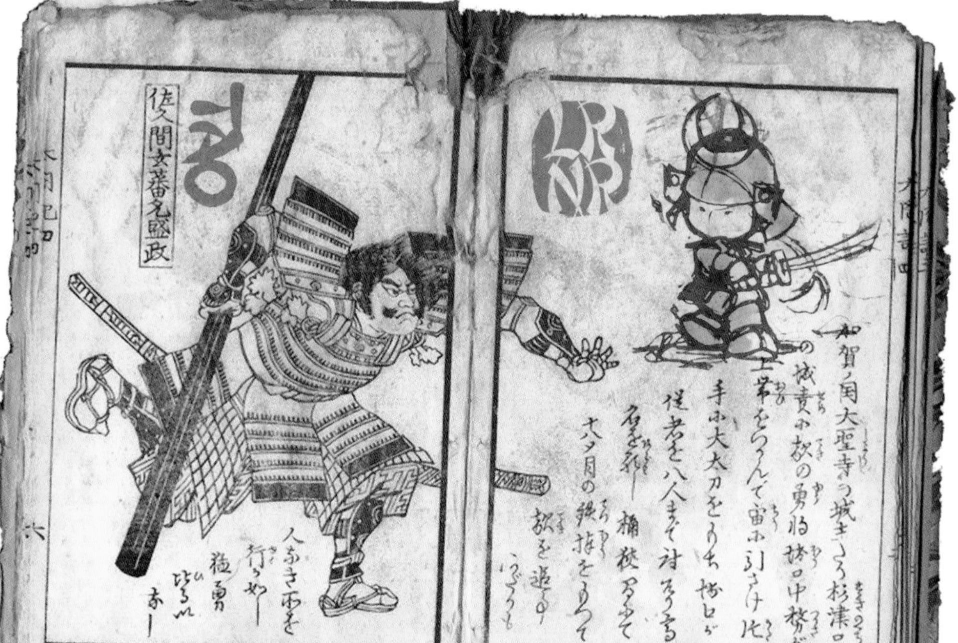
佐久間玄蕃允盛政

A True Ninja Leaves No Traces

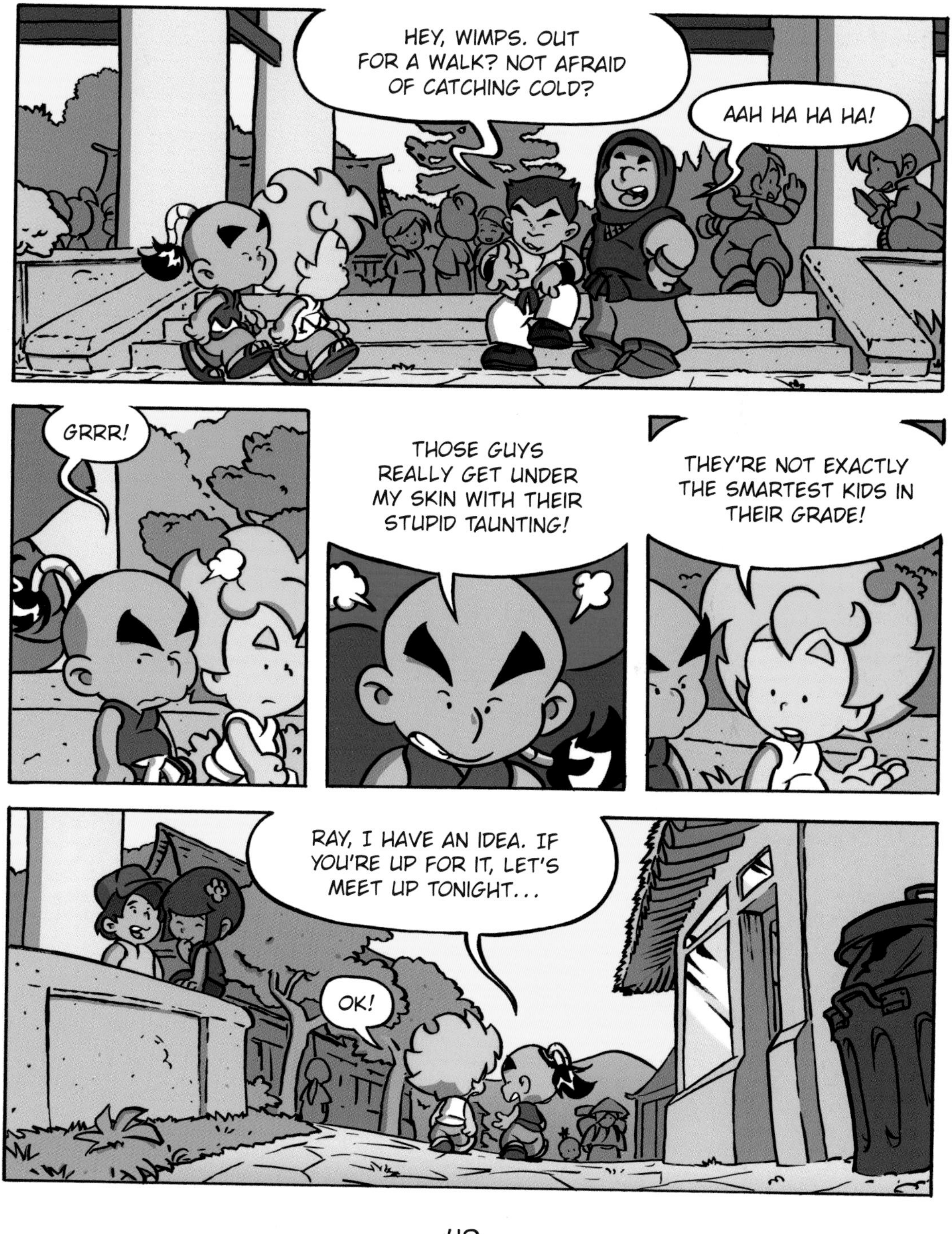
HEY, WIMPS. OUT FOR A WALK? NOT AFRAID OF CATCHING COLD?
AAH HA HA HA!
GRRR!
THOSE GUYS REALLY GET UNDER MY SKIN WITH THEIR STUPID TAUNTING!
THEY'RE NOT EXACTLY THE SMARTEST KIDS IN THEIR GRADE!
RAY, I HAVE AN IDEA. IF YOU'RE UP FOR IT, LET'S MEET UP TONIGHT...
OK!

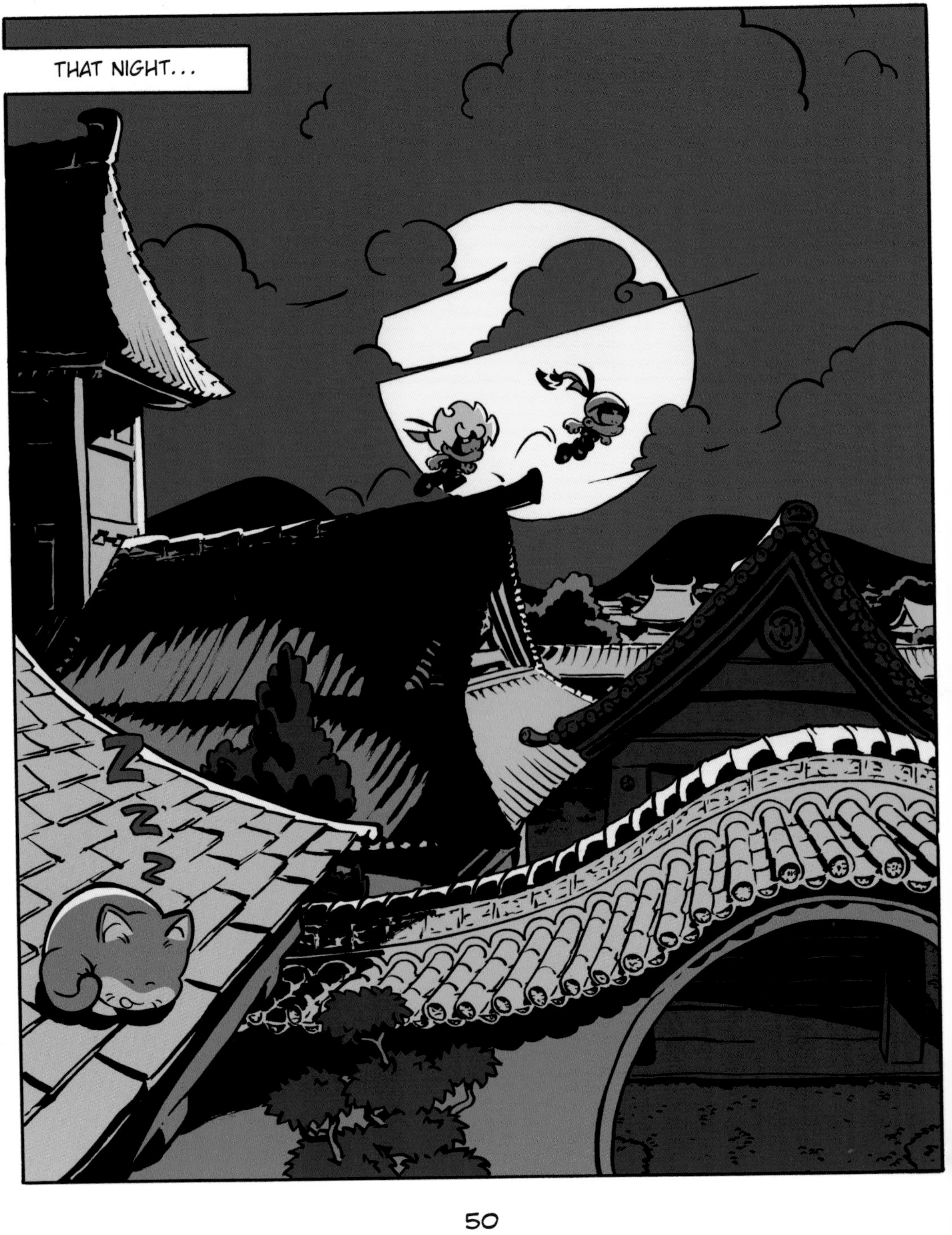
THAT NIGHT...
Z
Z
Z

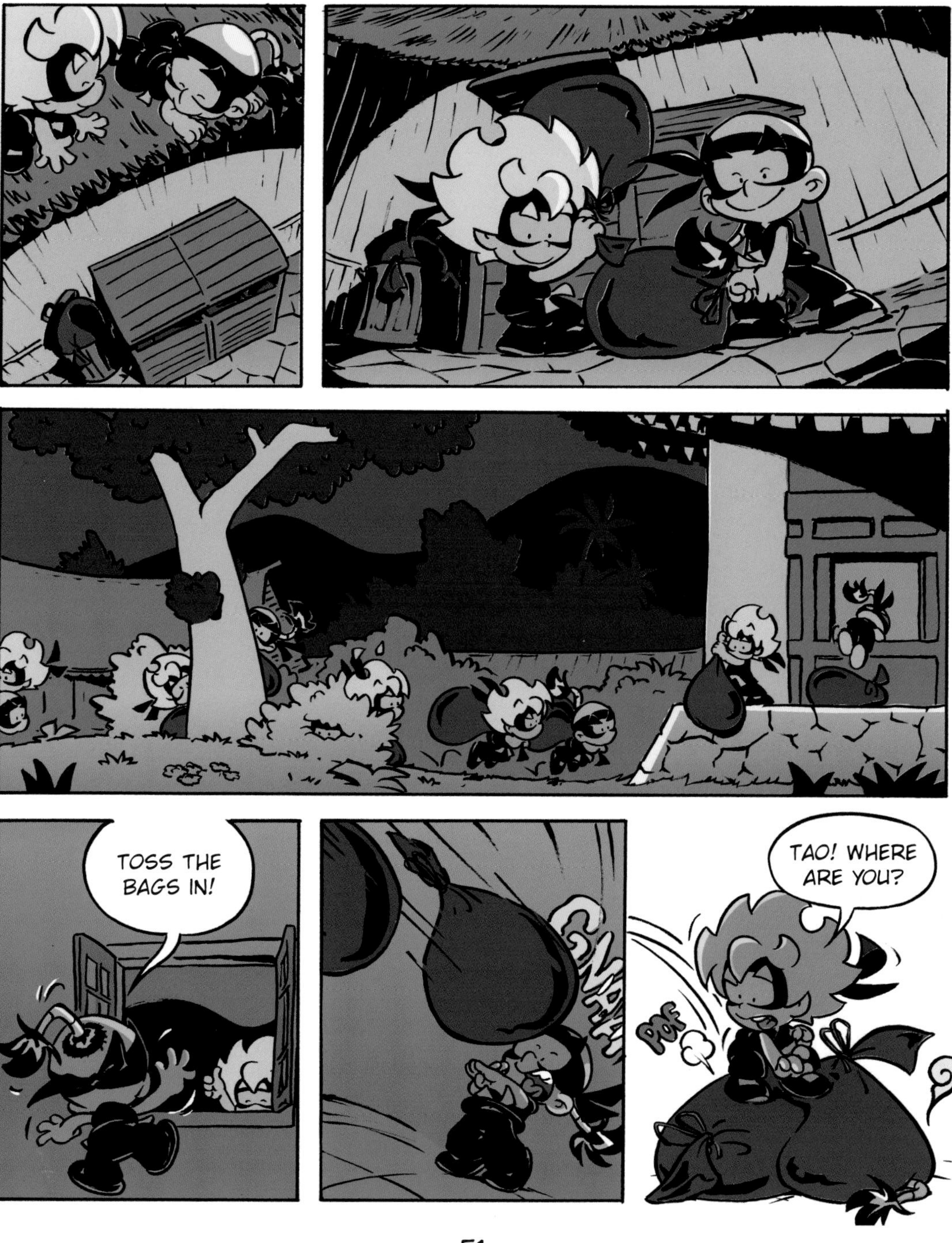
TOSS THE BAGS IN!
POF
TAO! WHERE ARE YOU?

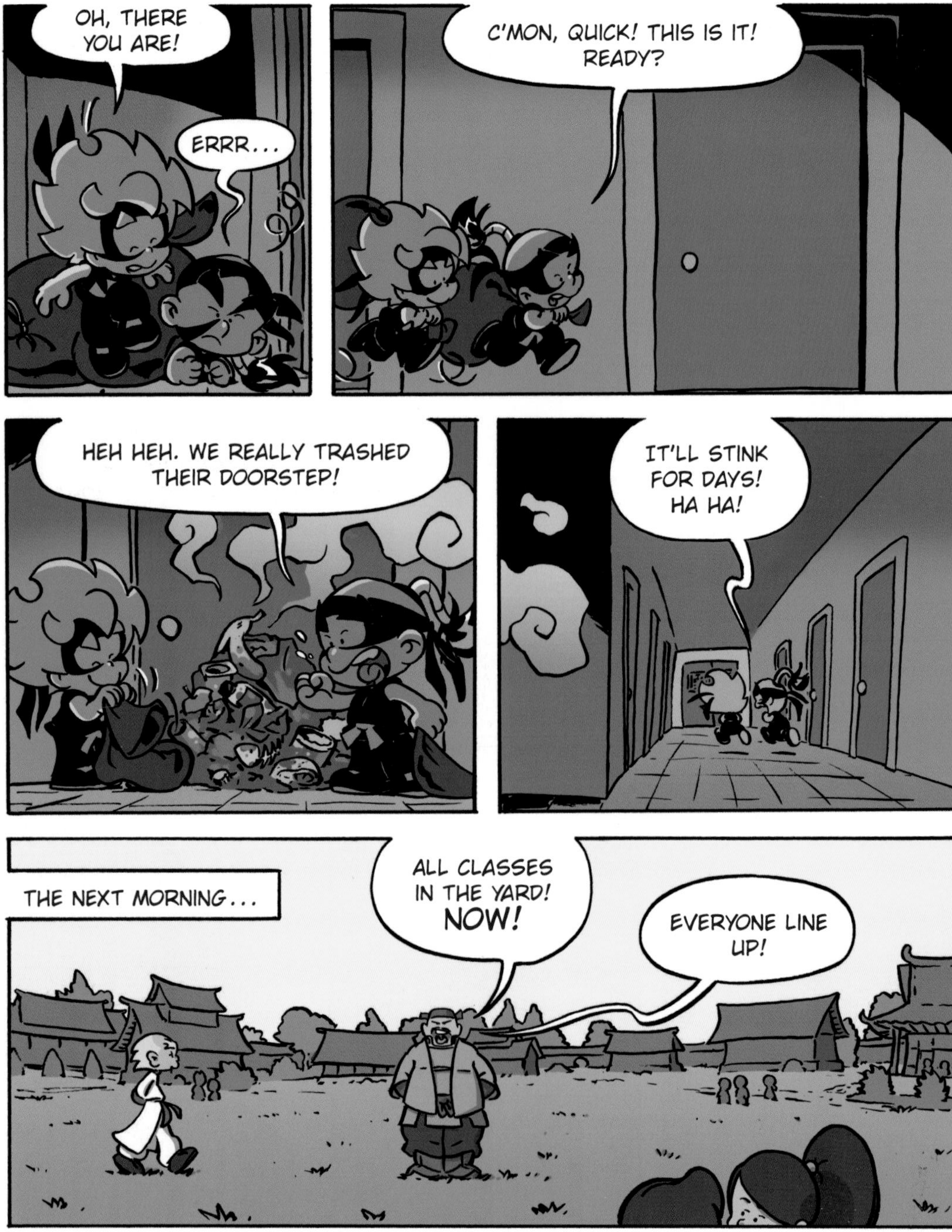
OH, THERE YOU ARE!
ERRR...
C'MON, QUICK! THIS IS IT! READY?
HEH HEH. WE REALLY TRASHED THEIR DOORSTEP!
IT'LL STINK FOR DAYS! HA HA!
THE NEXT MORNING...
ALL CLASSES IN THE YARD! NOW!
EVERYONE LINE UP!

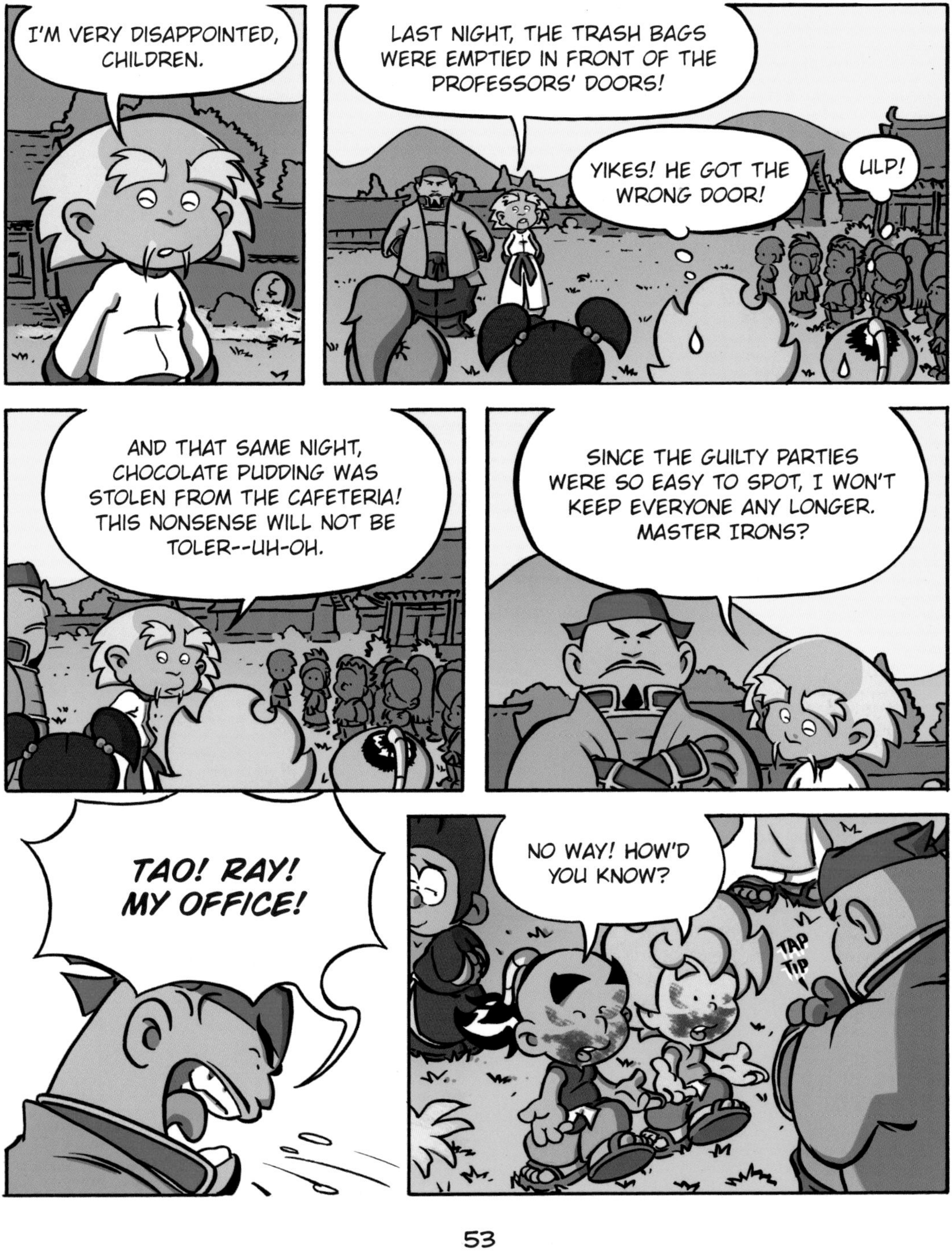
I'M VERY DISAPPOINTED, CHILDREN.
LAST NIGHT, THE TRASH BAGS WERE EMPTIED IN FRONT OF THE PROFESSORS' DOORS!
YIKES! HE GOT THE WRONG DOOR!
ULP!
AND THAT SAME NIGHT, CHOCOLATE PUDDING WAS STOLEN FROM THE CAFETERIA! THIS NONSENSE WILL NOT BE TOLER--UH-OH.
SINCE THE GUILTY PARTIES WERE SO EASY TO SPOT, I WON'T KEEP EVERYONE ANY LONGER. MASTER IRONS?
TAO! RAY! MY OFFICE!
NO WAY! HOW'D YOU KNOW?
TAP
TIP

Get ready for the next books in the Tao, the Little Samurai series!

#4

TAO
The Little Samurai
The Championship!
#4
Laurent Richard
Illustrated by Nicolas Ryser
GRAPHIC UNIVERSE

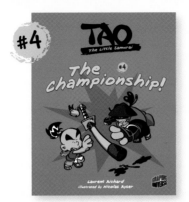

THE CHAMPIONSHIP!

When two top students from Master Snow's school disappear, Tao and his friends are on the case! This book-length Tao adventure has mysteries, a clan of nasty criminals, and a hunt for a legendary sword!

#5

TAO
The Little Samurai
Wild Animals!
#5
Laurent Richard
Illustrated by Nicolas Ryser
GRAPHIC UNIVERSE

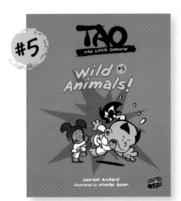

WILD ANIMALS!

A new student has arrived at Master Snow's school—and she has a crush on Tao! Meanwhile, Tao is teaching his little brother how to take care of bullies. He's also teaching his cat some ninja attacks!

TAO
The Little Samurai

#1 Pranks and Attacks!
#2 Ninjas and Knock Outs!
#3 Clowns and Dragons!